"I'll never get used to the miracle of birth. It's the perfect expression of God's magnificence," Ward said, gently stroking the newborn foal.

The mare rose to her feet, and in a few minutes, Princess tried her long wobbly legs without success.

"Why don't you get up and help her?" Shannon asked.

He shook his head. "She'll do it herself when she's ready. That's the wonderful thing about letting nature have its way. Everything has perfect timing if we will just keep the faith. If we try to force things, we end up in trouble."

A few minutes later, Princess stood on her wobbly legs. Calico moved close to her, allowing her baby to nurse.

The moving scene brought tears to Shannon's eyes.

"I know it's beautiful," Ward said, his own voice husky. The moment was a precious one, and as he looked at Shannon's rapturous expression, he knew with a strange sense of certainty there was no woman in the world with whom he'd rather share it.

Books by Leona Karr

Love Inspired

Rocky Mountain Miracle #131
Hero in Disguise #171
Hidden Blessing #194

LEONA KARR

A native of Colorado, Leona (Lee) Karr is the author of nearly forty books. Her favorite genres are inspirational romance and romantic suspense. Graduating from the University of Colorado with a B.A. and the University of Northern Colorado with an M.A. degree, she taught as a reading specialist until her first book was published in 1980. She has been on the Waldenbooks bestseller list and nominated by *Romantic Times* for Best Romantic Saga and Best Gothic Author. She has been honored as the Rocky Mountain Fiction Writer of the Year and received Colorado's Romance Writer of the Year Award. Her books have been reprinted in more than a dozen foreign countries. She is a presenter at numerous writing conferences and has taught college courses in creative writing.

Hidden Blessing
Leona Karr

Published by Steeple Hill Books™

STEEPLE HILL BOOKS

Steeple
Hill™

ISBN 0-373-87201-1

HIDDEN BLESSING

Copyright © 2002 by Leona Karr

Visit us at www.steeplehill.com

Printed in U.S.A.

I will give you a new heart
and put a new spirit within you.
—*Ezekiel* 36:26

With love to Debbie, Charlotte, Kay and Vivian.
My special family, and loyal fans.

Chapter One

The last thing that Shannon Hensley expected when she rented a summer cottage near Beaver Junction, Colorado, was to be confronted with a life-threatening forest fire.

"They're bringing in firefighters from all over," Isabel Watkins, the owner of the town's one grocery store, told Shannon as she quickly sacked her purchases. "This place is going to be worse than a beehive turned upside down."

Shannon's gray-blue eyes widened. "The report I heard said the fire was somewhere in the high country."

"That's us," Isabel replied with a nod. "The fire started up on the north ridge. They don't know if it was started by careless campers or lightning. Everyone was hoping that it would burn itself out, but the winds have spread the blaze downward.''

''But it's still miles away, isn't it?'' Shannon asked, feeling an unbidden quiver of nervousness. She'd rented a summer cottage in a deeply wooded area about fifteen miles from this small settlement and had only been settled a short time.

''Not many miles as the crow flies. It's unbelievable how fast a wildfire can spread,'' Isabel answered, shaking her head. ''They're hoping to get a fire line set up before the flames crest Prospect Ridge. Once it jumps into those thick drifts on the downhill slopes, it could make its way into this valley.''

Great, just great! Shannon thought, and filled with all kinds of misgivings, she left the store and started driving down the two-block Main Street. She'd driven to Colorado, looking for a quiet retreat where she could try to make some sense out of the shambles of her life. She had wanted to leave all the drama and trauma behind in Los Angeles. Even now she couldn't believe that she was jobless, friendless and facing another uphill battle to secure a prosperous future for herself.

It wasn't fair, but then she reminded herself that she'd never expected life to be fair. She'd fought tooth and nail for everything she'd ever gotten. Her parents had believed that looking out for number one was what life was all about and had taught their daughter well. Shannon's focus had been on climbing the corporate ladder since college, and there had been little time in her life for anything or anyone else. She was well on her way to achieving her high goals when, almost overnight, her high-paying position was eliminated because of a corporate takeover, and she was tossed out by new management as easily as they were replacing old office furnishings with new.

Now it seemed that her hopes of spending some relaxing downtime in Colorado were threatening to go up in smoke. Maybe she should pack up her things and get out of the area. Better to forgo a month's rent than put herself under more tension worrying about a forest fire driving her out. But where would she go? Her finances were tight at the moment, and the added expense of seeking out another retreat wasn't something she had planned on. Besides, she told herself firmly, the fire might never get within miles of her rented place. She decided that it wouldn't hurt to hang around for a couple of days even though this mountain valley was isolated with only one two-lane road leading from the Junction to a major highway in Elkhorn, a town about fifty miles away.

As Shannon turned onto the narrow road snaking up to her mountain cottage and other dwellings built on the slopes of Rampart Mountain, she braked to a sudden stop.

"What in the world?" She couldn't believe it. A wooden barricade was stretched across the road, and a man wearing a cowboy hat and Western clothes moved quickly to her car window. Under different circumstances she might have appreciated his strong masculine features and the way his brown eyes reflected a smile as he waited for her to lower the window on the driver's side. She guessed him to be somewhere in his early thirties as he gave a polite tip to his broad-brimmed Stetson and acknowledged her with a polite hello.

"What's going on?" she asked without returning his smile. Used to big city runaround, she was ready to summon any argument necessary to avoid wasting time at a roadblock.

"We have to keep all traffic off this road," he replied in an easy, conversational tone, holding his smile.

"Why?"

"To keep it clear for the emergency vehicles."

That slow easy smile of his was getting on her nerves, and she resented a deep, stroking voice that undoubtedly could play havoc with most females—but not her. She wasn't some backwoods gal who was used to taking orders from any smiling man who happened to be around, nor about to meekly accept this inconvenience without a firm protest.

"I don't see any traffic," she said firmly, as if that should settle the matter.

"You will in just a few minutes. The first caravan of forest fighters will be here shortly with trucks and all kinds of fire-fighting equipment. They're going to establish a base camp just a couple of miles from here. This whole area is going to be under siege before long."

"Does that mean the road is going to be closed indefinitely?" Shannon's sharp mind suddenly shifted into gear. What would this mean to her? She'd been a successful businesswoman because of her ability to handle unexpected situations. With dogged determination she had always made certain that she didn't come out the loser.

"I couldn't say how long it will be closed. It depends upon how fast the fire moves up the other side of Prospect Mountain." His slow, unruffled tone increased her irritation.

"I don't see why you can't let me drive quickly up to my place."

"Because I have my orders not to let anyone up this road."

"Then you're some kind of officer?" Her skepticism was obvious in her tone as she glanced over his Western shirt as if looking for a badge.

"No, just an ordinary citizen doing my duty," he answered smoothly. "Ward Dawson's the name. Now if you'll back up to that wide spot and turn around, you can wait out the road closures in town."

She glared at him. "How long will that be?"

"Well, let's see." He shoved his cowboy hat back far enough for her to see shocks of cinnamon brown hair framing his nicely tanned face. "Not more than a month, I reckon."

"A month!" She echoed, horrified. Then she saw the twinkle in his eyes and gave him a glare that told him she didn't appreciate his humor.

Ward silently chuckled. She was a testy one, all right, and he couldn't help kidding her a little. The California license plates on her fancy sports car had told him a lot. She was a city gal, all right, and a downright attractive one with wavy hair the color of corn silk, petite features and flashing gray-blue eyes that snapped at him. He didn't know who she was, but she sure wasn't going to drive anywhere up this road if he had anything to do with it.

"Surely, you have to allow people to get back to their homes," she insisted, not willing to accept his authority. She'd had plenty of practice confronting male superiors when they'd tried to tell her she couldn't do something and had learned there were always ways to get around rules. "It doesn't make sense to shut down a road when it's the only one in the area."

"I'm sorry," he said, firmly. "But that's the way it is."

"Why all this inconvenience when the fire is miles away? If you want everyone to stay out of the way, just tell them to stay in their houses and off the roads until the firefighters are finished." She mellowed her tone as if she was just offering a helpful suggestion. "That makes a lot more sense, doesn't it?"

Ward searched her face, almost sure she was putting him on, but her steady gaze was clear. Didn't she realize that it was anybody's guess whether they could get a handle on the fire before it crested the ridge and threatened this hillside and all the scattered homes on it? The fire was moving at an alarming rate in three different directions. He was tempted to set her straight that there might not be any homes to return to if the worst scenario came to pass. He decided that frightening her wasn't going to help anyone.

"They're setting up some accommodations at the school gym for people evicted from their homes," he told her with a firmness in his tone that didn't invite any further argument. "Do you know where the high school is? You can't miss it. It's a redbrick building—"

"With a sign that says Beaver High School? I think I can manage to find it," she said sarcastically. The small settlement of Beaver Junction would scarcely take up a three-block area in Los Angeles.

"Well, if you get lost you can always flag somebody down."

Pulling her car in reverse, the woman made a quick turn and headed toward Beaver Junction.

Watching her car disappear down the narrow road, Ward let out a deep laugh. She was a fiery one, all right, might be worth getting to know if things were different. But in the developing emergency, he'd be surprised if he ever saw her again.

As Shannon drove to the Junction, she mentally rehearsed all the things she'd say to him if she ever got the chance. When she reached the high school, she saw with a sinking heart that the parking lot was nearly full. All kinds of vehicles were vying for parking spaces. She was lucky to find an end spot for her small car.

After turning off the engine, Shannon sat for several minutes, listening to a Denver radio news station giving details of the rapidly moving wildfire. She searched the sky and could see a haze of smoke beyond the front range of mountains that cupped the valley. The radio report affirmed that all mountain roads in the threatened areas were restricted to emergency vehicles.

After hearing the news broadcast, Shannon decided the irritating Ward Dawson policing the road had only been following instructions. She felt a little ashamed of her assumption that he was just some local throwing his weight around. She could even forgive him his little joke of telling her it might be a month before the road was open.

Surely, with a statewide alert, enough knowledgable firefighters would be able to put the fire out as quickly as it had begun. There was no reason to panic, she told herself. Sighing, she realized that she would just have to be patient and wait with the rest of these strangers.

Collecting her purse and bag of groceries, she left the car and followed the crowd inside the building. The Red Cross had arrived. Tables had been set up in the front hall with a cardboard sign that read, Register Here If You Are An Evacuee.

Am I? Shannon asked herself. She wasn't sure just what the identification implied. As far as she was concerned, she was someone waiting for the road to clear so she could get back to her rented cottage.

When Shannon explained her circumstances, a pleasant, ruddy-faced woman handed her a form to fill out. "Your friends and relatives can contact us to know you're safe," the volunteer explained.

For the first time, Shannon felt a quiver of foreboding that the situation might not be as quickly resolved as she had assumed. She wrote her name on the form and handed it to the woman without filling it out.

The lady volunteer raised an eyebrow. "Isn't there someone who needs to be notified about your safety?"

Shannon shook her head and walked away. Her insistence on independence and total privacy suddenly had a hollow ring to it. Even her closest former co-workers had no idea she had taken off for Colorado. She felt it was none of their business. No one would be waiting to hear from her. No friends or relatives would be inquiring after her safety.

Reluctantly, she joined the milling crowd in the gym

where clusters of people were busily talking, looking out windows, trying to placate crying children or sitting silently on cots that were being set up as quickly as they were delivered.

A tall, angular woman wearing a Red Cross pin spied Shannon carrying her small sack of groceries. She hurried over to her and gave Shannon a grateful smile.

"Oh, good, donated food. Here, let me take that sack to the cafeteria for you. God knows, every little bit will help. We have no idea how many will need to be fed tonight."

Shannon readily handed over the sack and watched the woman scurry away as if she held a treasure in her hand instead of a quart of milk, three bananas, a box of crackers and a six-pack of a diet drink. The idea of feeding all these men, women and children was more than Shannon could contemplate.

All over the crowded gym, people were talking quietly together. Others were fighting back tears or sitting silently as if in a state of shock. Most of the men were wearing work clothes, as if they'd been suddenly taken off some job, and the women wore casual summer tops with their slacks or jeans. Shannon felt more out of place than ever in her pale-yellow linen dress and matching designer sandals. Several puzzled glances came her way as she headed to a corner of the gym to sit down in a folding chair.

Announcements over the school's public address system blared in her ears, but most of the information had no relevance for her since she was unfamiliar with the names of places and people. Although she had a detached sympathy for the milling townspeople around her, she felt alien to them. As the hours passed, she decided that as soon as the roads opened to general traffic, she'd leave the area and forget about losing her three weeks rent on the mountain cottage.

Ward had forgotten all about the attractive blonde in the fancy sports car until later that evening when he brought some supplies to the high school. The place was a madhouse. Growing numbers of evacuated families from threatened and closed areas had poured into Beaver Junction all afternoon, seeking refuge at the school.

A call had gone out for cots, food and supplies, and Ward had made a quick trip to his ranch, located twenty miles up the mountain valley. He and his young ranch hand, Ted Thompson, had stripped the house of some extra cots and brought them to the school.

"You're God's own angel, Ward Dawson," the preacher's wife, Laura Cozzins, told him with a broad grin on her round face as she accepted his donations.

"That's what my mother always used to say." Ward nodded solemnly.

Laura laughed heartily. She was a small woman with greying short hair and a ready twinkle in her hazel eyes. "Glory, glory, we must not be thinking of the same God-loving woman. As much as your parents adored you, Ward, I don't ever remember them calling you an angel."

"Ah, come on, now, I wasn't that bad."

"No, you weren't." She grinned at him. "Just heading down the wrong road. It was a miracle, for sure, the way you made a U-turn when you came back to the ranch to live." Her smile faded a little. "I know it wasn't easy for you, but the Lord wasn't about to cut you free."

"Yep, He had a lasso on me, for sure," Ward admitted, remembering how hard he'd fought, trying to follow his destructive godless path in the college town where he'd been working. Both Laura and her husband had been there for him when he'd passed through his Gethsemane three years ago. After his wife, Valerie, had died and left him with an infant daughter to raise, he'd moved with Tara to the family ranch so that his older sister, Beth, could help raise his little girl. Since then, he'd learned to live in the moment and trust divine guidance to take care of the rest.

Ward gave Laura's plump shoulders a quick hug. "You're the prettiest gal around. If you weren't already taken, I'd throw my hat in the ring."

Laughing, she gave him a playful shove. "Your sweet talking is wasted on me. Now, you and Ted get busy setting up these cots before I think of some more work to keep the two of you out of trouble."

They had just finished that job when Ward spied the California woman sitting all by herself. Her apparent indifference to the plight of others around her was disappointing but not unfamiliar. When he'd gone off to college, he couldn't wait to leave home. Like the prodigal son, he'd thrown off all restraints and concern about others. Living campus life to the fullest, he forgot about the firm Christian values in which he'd been raised, and when he'd married his last year in college, it had been without any consideration except that he liked Valerie more than any girl he'd met, and they had a good time together. Her death when Tara was only two had left him emotionally bankrupt, and he'd come home to find himself. He didn't know what the emptiness in the pretty stranger's life might be, but he recognized the sign of a soul shut off from its source of peace and happiness.

"Do you know who that young woman is?" he asked his eighteen-year-old ranch hand, who usually had an eye out for any attractive female who wandered into town.

"Nope." Ted shook his curly black head. "Haven't seen her before. She must be new around here."

"I know she's staying at one of those summer homes on the north ridge," Ward offered. "She drives a fancy sports car with a California license, but that's all I know about her."

Ted grinned. "Well, if you're interested, boss, there's only one remedy for that. Go talk to her."

Ward wasn't sure that interested was the right word. Curious, perhaps. Responding to Ted's knowing grin, he took up the challenge. "You know something? I think I will."

Shannon had stayed pretty much to herself during the long hours of waiting, wandering aimlessly around the school or sitting in a corner of the gym. When she saw Ward coming in her direction, she instantly recognized him. Oh, no, she thought, silently, as he wove his way through the crowd toward her. Now that she understood the scope of the emergency, she was a little ashamed of herself for challenging his authority. Not that she was about to apologize. He'd been secretly laughing at her all the time, and she knew it.

He seemed to know just about everyone. She watched him scoop up a little girl for a quick hug, and a moment later he planted a kiss on the forehead of a grandmotherly lady. An attractive young woman dressed in western pants, a plaid shirt and cowboy boots pushed toward him and said something that made them both laugh. As Ward tweaked her chin in a playful fashion, she looked at him with a soft expression that betrayed a strong affection.

Watching them, Shannon was filled with an emotion she refused to identify as strangely akin to envy. Jerking her eyes in another direction, she scolded herself for being interested in this cowboy's personal life.

So he had a sweetheart or wife, so what?

"Hello, again." He greeted her with a warm familiarity as he suddenly stood in front of her. "I see you found the school all right."

Looking into his tanned face with its high cheekbones, firm straight nose and strong jawline, she was terribly aware of how much she wanted to mend fences with him. But she was equally determined to show him she wasn't some whimpering damsel in distress.

"It was a challenge," she answered lightly. "But I managed not to get lost."

"I suspect you always know where you're going."

"Yes, I do," she answered. If he was trying to get a rise out of her, she wasn't going for the bait. "I've heard rumors that the wind has shifted, and the roads might be opened in the morning."

He nodded. "Could be. I guess it depends on whether things stay the same during the night."

"And if they do?" she asked hopefully.

"Well, I reckon that they'll give the okay for people who live in the area to pay a quick visit to their homes. Most of them didn't have time to bring very much with them when they were ordered to vacate." He sobered. "It's not easy to decide what's important when you're under that kind of pressure."

"Are you one of the displaced?" she asked, wondering if he was personally involved or just volunteering to police the road.

"Nope, I'm one of the lucky ones. My ranch is farther up the valley. God willing, we'll be spared."

When he said, *we,* she glanced at his ring finger. No gold band. Feminine curiosity made her wonder who the young woman was who had hugged him with such ardor.

"Have you met any of the other folks?" he asked. Something about her obvious withdrawal from everyone around her challenged Ward to do something about it. "Why don't you let me introduce you around, Miss—"

"Shannon Hensley. Thanks, but I've decided to leave as soon as the main road opens, whether I can get my belongings from the rented cottage or not." Where she would go was another question, but she knew she wanted to see the last of Beaver Junction as quickly as possible.

"And you'll be heading back to California?"

"No. Not right away," she said, smothering a sigh. It was ironic, really, that she was sitting in a crowded gym with a bunch of homeless people and had no idea what she should do next. She'd spent a month applying to every high-tech company on the West Coast without even getting a nibble for a new position. She'd temporarily rented her expensive beachfront apartment, left her résumé with several employment agencies and made arrangements to come to Colorado to spend some quiet time. She wasn't about to admit to this stranger that she was without home, family or close friends. "I haven't made up my mind exactly where I'll go."

Her voice was firm enough, but Ward could see the shadow of worry in her attractive eyes, which seemed to constantly change colours from gray to smoky blue. She was wearing a dress in a shade of yellow that brought out sun-bleached highlights in her hair, and in his opinion, her figure was as eye-catching as any pictured on the cover of a woman's magazine. Why would such a California beauty end up alone in a place like Beaver Junction, he asked himself? He would have thought that fancy resorts in Aspen or Vail would be more her style.

"Do you need to let your family or anyone know that you're all right?" he asked, in an obvious attempt to learn more about her personal background.

"No, there's no one," she replied quickly. "Since my parents died, I only have one aunt I communicate with once in a while. Thank you, but I can handle this situation nicely by myself."

Her lovely chin jutted out at a belligerent angle, and he hid a smile. There was something of a stubborn child about her that both appealed to him and irritated him. "There's no need to be afraid—"

"I'm not afraid." She flared at the insinuation. "I just want to get out of this place as quickly as I can. One night cooped up here with all these people will be all I can take."

"I see. Well, good night then," he said politely. Her apparent indifference to the plight of others around her sparked the urge to handle her the way he would a stubborn mare. It was a good thing she wasn't going to be around long enough for a battle of wills.

Left alone, Shannon had a moment of regret that she hadn't kept him talking to her. Nobody else had tried to strike up a conversation with her all afternoon. She knew they were caught up in the perils of their situation, and even though she sympathized with their worries and anguish, she wasn't up to all the commotion and crush of humanity crowded together, breathing the same air and having no privacy. The whole situation was some kind of unbelievable nightmare.

As Shannon's eyes followed Ward's tall figure across the gym, she saw him stop to talk to a plump, gray-haired woman. During their conversation, the woman nodded, and her gaze darted in Shannon's direction. Shannon was positive they were talking about her.

She stiffened. What was Ward Dawson telling the woman? How dare he repeat any of their conversation? She knew then that she shouldn't have revealed so much about her family situation and indefinite plans. Shannon began simmering. She was an outsider, and fair game for the rumor mills. She could imagine what fun the small-town gossips would have speculating about her private affairs.

Shannon braced herself when Ward left the gym, and the woman to whom he'd been talking made her way purposefully toward her. Shannon knew then that her suspicions had been right.

"Hi, I'm Laura Cozzins, the reverend's wife," the woman said, introducing herself in a friendly, breezy manner that matched the smile on her broad face. "Sorry I haven't had time to say hello before now. Ward told me he's a friend of yours and that you'd love to help us in the cafeteria. We'll be setting out some food pretty soon now, and I'm grateful that you've volunteered to help."

Volunteered to help? Shannon was speechless and utterly aghast at the number of lies Ward Dawson had squeezed into one sentence. He wasn't a friend, nothing had been said about her helping, and she hadn't volunteered for anything.

"Come on, dear, and I'll show where the kitchen is." Laura smiled at Shannon. "We've really got our hands full. The Red Cross ladies are doing all they can, but more displaced families are arriving all the time. Two more hands will be a great help, and God bless you for offering to help."

Shannon managed a weak smile. Telling the preacher's wife the truth would have been too embarrassing under the circumstances. She rose to her feet and followed the preacher's wife into a hot, crowded kitchen.

For the next two hours, Shannon cut up a gigantic mound of potatoes for French fries, cooked them in boiling oil, then served them to a seemingly never-ending line of refugees.

She was hot, sweating and had aching muscles by the time all the stranded families had finished eating. When it was time for the volunteer help to sit down at the tables, Shannon had little appetite left. Ignoring the food that had been prepared, she searched the kitchen and found one of the bananas that had been in her confiscated grocery sack.

Like a fugitive escaping, she slipped out the kitchen door. Outside the building, a night breeze bathed her perspiring face with blessed relief. A faint glow on the far horizon marred the dark night sky, and the cool air was tinged with the odor of burned wood. As she walked around the building, eating her banana and enjoying the blessing of being alone, she prayed that the wind was blowing the fire back on itself.

She didn't see the small figure on the sidewalk ahead of her until she heard a childish voice calling in a whisper.

"Pokey! Pokey, where are you?"

As she came closer she saw a little boy about four years old standing in the middle of the walk. When he heard Shannon's footsteps, he turned quickly and came running up to her.

"What's the matter?" she asked, seeing his tear-streaked face.

"Have you seen my puppy dog? His name is Pokey. He's black with white paws, and not very big."

"No, I'm sorry, I haven't," she said gently. "Did he get loose?"

"We left him behind. He didn't come when Mama called. She said we couldn't wait to find him."

"Oh, I'm sorry," Shannon said. Pokey must have lived up to his name one too many times, and had been left behind. Even though she'd never had any pets of her own, she could certainly sympathize with the loss of one. She felt the youngster's anguish and tried to console him as best she could.

"I'm sure he'll be all right," Shannon said, not really being sure about anything at the moment.

"I know Pokey would find me if…if he knew where I was."

"He's probably just waiting for you to come back home."

"When can we go home?" the child sobbed, asking the question that was in both their minds. "I want to go home now."

"I know." She brushed a shock of brown hair from his forehead.

"I don't like it here."

Me, neither, Shannon added silently.

She spoke with more conviction than she felt. "I'm sure they'll have the fire put out soon. Now, we'd better go inside. Your mother will be looking for you."

Even as she spoke, they could hear a woman's strident voice calling, "Kenny. Kenny. Where are you?"

Shannon took the child's hand and led him to a worried and anxious young mother.

"Oh, thank God," she breathed. "You scared the living daylights out of me, Kenny. I've been hunting everywhere for you. You know you're supposed to stay inside unless we're with you."

"He was looking for his dog," Shannon said quickly, trying to help the little boy out. "He's worried about Pokey being left behind."

"I know," the mother said wearily. "The dog didn't come when we called and called, so we had no choice but to leave without him. Our home is one of the highest on the mountain." Her lips trembled. "We couldn't take time to hunt for Pokey. We barely had time to collect Kenny, the baby and pack a few belongings. The road is still closed, and we can't go back until they say so."

"Maybe tomorrow they'll open it, at least for a little while," Shannon offered hopefully. "I guess it depends upon the wind."

Kenny's mother nodded. "I'm Alice Gordon." She smiled when Shannon introduced herself. "I'm glad to meet you, Shannon. We're all praying they'll get the fire out before it makes it over Prospect Ridge." Shannon could see her lips quiver as she took her son's hand. "Thank the Lord, we're all safe here."

She disappeared inside the building, leaving Shannon alone. Not wanting to go inside, Shannon continued along the sidewalk that led to the parking lot at the far side of the school.

She slowed her steps when she reached the lot and was about to turn around when she saw Ward heading for a pickup truck parked nearby.

Shannon was debating whether to call to him and give him a piece of her mind when he glanced back and saw her in the glow of one of the high arc lights.

He waved, then came quickly over to where she was standing. "I wondered where you'd gone. Hiding out, are you?'' he chided with that easy teasing smile of his.

"Should I be?'' she countered, still debating how she wanted to handle this infuriating man. "Have you decided to volunteer me for something else?''

He raised an eyebrow. "Not a good idea, huh?''

"Frankly, I don't appreciate someone manipulating me like that.''

"Sorry, I thought that it would do you good just to mix a little bit with the others.''

"Thank you for your concern, but I'm perfectly capable of looking out for myself. Good night, Mr. Dawson.''

"Wait a minute.'' Her cool and dismissing manner was a new experience for him. Ward wasn't used to having any female, young or old, treat him with such cold indifference. None of the women he'd dated since Valerie's death had come close to leading him to the altar. He'd given the reins of his life over to God, and so far, he hadn't found anyone who held to the same spiritual values. A deep Christian dedication had been absent in his first marriage, and he wouldn't make that mistake again. He didn't know why he felt the need to challenge this stubborn, self-assured woman, but he did. Even though she'd made it plain that she didn't appreciate his interference, he couldn't help chipping away at her crisp edges.

"Laura said she appreciated the help and told me to thank you. You know, it's going to take all of us pulling together to get through this thing.''

His clothes were dusty and wrinkled. Fatigue had

deepened the strong lines in his face. Shannon wondered how many jobs he'd taken on.

"I really didn't mind all that much," she admitted. "But you would never have volunteered me for kitchen work if you knew what a disaster I am when it comes to cooking."

"I guess that was pretty nervy of me," he admitted with a wry smile. "I just thought things might be easier for you if you mixed a little bit with the others."

"No harm done," she said, suddenly contrite. She was ashamed for misjudging him. "What do you think my chances are of getting back to my place tomorrow to pack up my things?"

He surprised her by answering, "Actually, I think there's a good chance. The weathermen are predicting that the wind shift is going to last until at least tomorrow night."

"Really? That's wonderful." She almost clapped her hands.

Ward was stunned at how lovely and suddenly alive and beautiful she was. In the shadow of the building, she seemed like some kind of heavenly specter in her soft yellow dress and shiny hair. An undefined jolt shot through him as she smiled broadly at him for the first time, and something deep inside responded on a level that made no earthly sense at all.

Chapter Two

A ripple of excitement and relief moved through the cafeteria the next morning when a fire chief stood in front of the refugees and announced, "All of you who have homes below Prospect Ridge will be allowed back in the area for a two-hour period." He emphasized the time limit. "Two hours only. You got that?" His steely eyes dragged around the room. "The wind could shift at any time, and anyone still on the mountain could be caught in a fiery downdraft. Concentrate on speedily collecting the necessities, and let the rest go. Understand?"

There was a murmur of agreement from the crowd, and as Shannon bounded out of the building with the other evacuees, her mind raced. Two hours! That was enough time to get herself cleaned up with a quick shower and a change of clothes, with time left over to pack all her belongings in the car. Once the highway was open to general traffic, she'd leave Beaver Junction as fast as she could. Just where she would go to find the quiet retreat she needed was something she'd have to decide later. Right now, her pressing need was to get out of the present situation as soon as she could.

As she drove away from the school, she felt a pang of sympathy for those who would have to remain and endure a heartrending vigil, not knowing if their homes would be spared. She already felt drained and off balance.

A line of cars trailing out of town and up the side of the mountain moved at a snail's pace, and Shannon's agitation grew as precious time slipped away. A heavy haze of smoke billowed into the sky from some point hidden beyond Prospect Ridge, and her nostrils quivered with the pungent odor of burning wood. Her chest tightened as she realized that thick drifts of aspen and pine trees on each side of the road promised more fuel for the greedy fire if it topped the ridge and came racing downward. She clutched the steering wheel with nervous hands as she drove up the side of the mountain, forced to take the serpentine curves slowly instead of with her usual speed.

By the time she pulled into the driveway of the rented mountain cottage, she had lost more than a half hour of her precious time limit. She raced into the small house, and before she did anything else, she went directly to the telephone and dialed the employment agency that had sent out her applications. She had tried to use her cell phone, but it had kept fading out on her.

Her mouth went dry as she waited for someone to answer. Common sense told her it was too soon to expect any results, but she might get lucky, and if anyone was interested in interviewing her this soon, she could immediately head to California. Her pragmatic nature desperately needed a definite course of action. She had never been able to stand not having a specific agenda, and her present situation had heightened a need to get back in charge of her life.

"I'm sorry, Miss Hensley, we don't have anything right now, but I'm sure it's just a matter of time," a pleasant woman advised her after Shannon had made her inquiry.

Time. Shannon bit her lip. Patience had never been one of her most admirable qualities. In fact, she knew that impatience with herself, others and the world in general had been a driving force in her life, but she also knew she hadn't accomplished her climb in the business world by wasting time. She was proud of her reputation as a hardheaded businesswoman, and at the moment, she felt even more driven because her life was at a standstill.

"I would appreciate your doing everything you can to facilitate my applications," Shannon said as calmly as she could. She wasn't about to reveal the anxious tremors she felt inside.

"I can reach you at this number, can't I? If something should develop?" asked the lady in her professional, optimistic voice.

Shannon hesitated. Rather than go into the long explanation of the fire and her predicament, she answered, "I'm not sure, but I'll call you frequently and keep in touch."

When Shannon hung up, she sat for a long minute. Maybe she should start concentrating on finding a position in another part of the country. She hated to leave the Los Angeles area, but if nothing developed in the next few weeks, she'd have to relocate and find a position elsewhere, anyway. She'd only rented her apartment on a temporary basis, but the couple who had taken it would probably sign an extended lease, or maybe even buy it. She ran a tired hand through her hair. Just thinking about giving up all that she'd struggled to create for herself brought a bone-deep weariness and anger. It wasn't fair.

She glanced at her watch, then stood up with a jerk. She couldn't believe how fast the time was going. Hurriedly, she stripped off her wrinkled clothes and dived into the shower, delighting in the cleansing sprays of warm water. Although they had opened the gym showers at the school to the displaced refugees, Shannon had declined to push her way into the line of people waiting to use them. Personal privacy had always been important to her, and having been raised in an affluent family as the only child, she'd always enjoyed her own things and her own space.

She sighed with utter contentment as she bathed with her favorite scented soap and shampooed her hair. She stepped out of the shower, refreshed, and quickly dressed in tailored slacks and a matching soft blue knit top. She towel-dried her shoulder-length hair and secured it in a clip at the back of her head.

She deliberately ignored the moving hands on her watch as she began packing her suitcases, giving careful attention to a small canvas overnight bag that she would keep with her. She hadn't unpacked the boxes that had held her books and laptop computer. She took them out to the car and stowed them in the trunk, along with her suitcases. She made one last trip to fill some kitchen sacks with foodstuff she didn't want to leave behind.

When she was ready to lock the front door of the cottage, she dared a look at her watch. She couldn't believe it! Already a half hour past the two-hour limit. Lifting her head, she quickly searched the mountain skyline. There seemed to be more dark smoke thickening on the horizon.

She bounded down the front steps, opened the door to her car and was about to climb in when she heard some commotion behind her. She swung around. A small black dog with white feet scurried toward her, his tail wagging furiously as he greeted her enthusiastically with a friendly, puppy-size bark.

There was no doubt in Shannon's mind that he was Pokey. She laughed as the puppy danced around her feet and put his paws on her legs. As she picked the fellow up, his little legs shot out in all directions, and his pink tongue was like windshield wipers gone berserk as he washed her face with jubilant kisses.

"I know someone who's going to be glad to see you," she said, chuckling as she opened the back door of the car and put him inside. "Lie down, Pokey," she ordered, but the puppy stood on the back seat, his head cocked to one side and his tail wagging as fiercely as ever.

She tossed her shoulder purse on top of her small overnight bag and hurriedly backed out of the gravel driveway.

There was no sign of other cars on the narrow winding road ahead, and she kept glancing in the mirror to see if there were any stragglers behind her. The road was pointedly empty. She couldn't believe everyone else had observed the time limit. Well, it didn't matter. Once traffic was allowed on the highway to Elkhorn, she'd be on her way out of here.

She was lost in thought when suddenly, without warning, Pokey suddenly leaped from the back seat into the front, sending her purse and the small canvas overnight bag flying.

"No, Pokey, no!" she protested as the dog tried to scramble into her arms. In her effort to shove him away, she turned the steering wheel too sharply.

The car left the pavement.

Frantically she tried to bring it back on the road, but the wheels failed to gain any traction on the narrow dirt shoulder. The car began to slowly slide downward.

Panic-stricken, she fumbled with her seat belt. Before she could get it unfastened, the car sounded as if its insides were being torn out, and it stopped with a jolt that threw her forward. Only her seat belt kept her from crashing her head against the dashboard.

What was happening? The back end of the car slanted downward, and the road lay about fifty yards above. Any moment she expected the car to start sliding again.

The dog was dancing all over the seat, trying to get into her arms. "No, Pokey, we have to get out."

The door wouldn't open. She shoved as hard as she could, but it was wedged shut. She saw then that none of the doors would open wide enough for her to get out. All were jammed against huge boulders that had momentarily snagged the car.

She was trapped, and even the slightest movement seemed to rock the car on its precarious perch.

Ward glanced at his watch for the tenth time in less than five minutes. He was positioned at the bottom of the mountain road, checking off the names of residents who had homes in that area. Every name had been crossed off his list but one, Shannon Hensley.

"Why am I not surprised?" he asked himself. She was already an hour late. As he waited at the checkpoint, his irritation and disappointment over her disregard for instructions turned into just plain anger.

Knowing he was needed in a dozen different places, he answered his cell phone curtly when it rang, "Dawson, here."

"Everybody off the mountain, Ward?" asked one of the fire chiefs watching Prospect Ridge.

"Not quite. We've got one left. A woman."

The chief muttered something under his breath. "We've got trouble up here. The wind's shifting, and our fire line on the ridge may not hold. If the sparks jump across the ridge, the whole mountain could be threatened. Get her out of there if you have to drag her."

"Right. I'll get on it."

"I'll bring her down kicking and screaming if I have to," Ward said under his breath as he climbed into his pickup truck and headed up the mountain, driving at a speed only someone who knew the road would dare.

As Ward silently rehearsed all the sharp things he

was going to say to her, he was suddenly filled with a strange impulse to slow down. He'd learned to trust an inner voice that often guided him when he needed it most, and paying heed to it at that moment proved to be a blessing once again. If he'd been driving at his former speed, he would have whipped right by the white car that was off the road without even seeing it. As it was, he glanced down the slope of the rocky hillside and did a double take.

"What in the—" He slammed on his brakes. He couldn't believe what he was seeing. The fancy white sports car was precariously hung up on a shelf of large boulders a good distance below the road. Only rocks and low shrubs dotted the hillside.

Bounding from the truck, he started down the steep slope, slipping and sliding all the way. He fought to keep his balance as he scrambled over loose rocks and thickets of scrub oak.

The closer he came to the car, the tighter his chest got. He saw that by some miracle, it was caught precariously in the midst of some large boulders. If the boulders hadn't been there, there would have been nothing to stop the car's plunge into the deep ravine below.

"Thank you, Lord," he breathed.

Even before he reached the car, he began to weigh the situation. How deeply were the rocks rooted in the ground? How long would they hold against the heavy downward pull of the car? Could he get Shannon out without disturbing the precarious balance that held the automobile? As these questions flashed through his mind, he saw another complication. Huge rocks hugged the sides of the car.

Shannon's stricken pale face was clearly visible through the windshield. As he neared the car, she waved frantically to him as if he might suddenly decide to go away.

He was sure his eyes were deceiving him when he saw what looked like a dog in the seat with her. She hadn't said anything about having a pet.

As he peered through the driver's window, he gave her as much of a reassuring smile as he could manage and said loudly, "It's going to be okay. I'll get you out as fast as I can."

He didn't have an answer for the question he saw in her eyes. He surveyed the car. He knew at any moment the whole shelf of rocks could pull out from the ground, and everything would start sliding. One thing was certain. There wasn't any time to waste.

He was concerned that shifting even one of the boulders could affect the balance of the others. Very gingerly, he began putting his weight against one of the rocks pinning the front door shut.

Lord, lend me Your strength and wisdom. And I could even use an angel or two, right now.

After painstaking effort, only one large boulder remained against the front door on the driver's side. Ward breathed another prayer as he put his full weight against it. Slowly the rock began to move, and then, with one momentous shove, he sent it rolling with a crash down the slope. Afraid that the movement could have loosened the other rocks, he jerked open the door.

"Get out quickly," he ordered. He knew that they

had to get away from the car as soon as possible, in case the shelf of rocks broke away under their feet.

The dog scrambled out first, leaping over Shannon. When Ward saw that she was getting out, hanging onto her purse and a small suitcase, he barked, "Drop everything and climb as fast as you can."

In Shannon's shaken state, leaving all her belongings in the car and trunk was devastating. She ignored his order to drop her purse and overnight bag.

When Ward saw the stubborn set of her mouth, he grabbed the suitcase from her. "Move." He gave her a not-too-gentle shove forward. With the dog bounding ahead of them, they scrambled up the steep slope.

Shannon was breathing heavily when they reached the shoulder of the road. Her whole body shook when she looked at the car, which so easily could have been a heap of crushed metal at the bottom of the ravine— with her in it! Tears flooded her eyes, and her lips trembled. She'd never had a brush with death before, and when she felt Ward's arm go around her shoulder, she leaned into him, grateful for the warmth of his strong body that lessened a threatening hysteria within her.

"It's all right," he soothed. "You're okay." *Thank you, Lord,* Ward prayed. He gently stroked her back, and a swelling of tenderness took him totally by surprise. He didn't understand why this woman he scarcely knew could create such a deep stirring in him. They had no common ground to build even a slight friendship, and he was certain that in any other situation, she would only be slightly amused by his presence. And yet, as she trembled in his arms, he wanted more than anything to kiss away the tears on her cheeks and bring a smile to her.

"I'm sorry," she murmured, drawing away and swiping at her tears. Shannon kept her head lowered and didn't look at him. Anybody with eyes in their head ought to be able to drive down an empty road without running off it. She'd always prided herself on her perfect driving record, and now this!

"Nothing to be sorry about," he reassured her. "You're safe—that's all that matters. I think we ought to get going. I don't like the looks of that sky."

Pokey had been bouncing around at their feet, woofing excitedly as if the world was a wonderful place when people were around to keep him company.

"Come on, pup," Ward said as he and Shannon moved toward the pickup. Without waiting for an invitation, Pokey jumped in and settled happily on Shannon's lap.

Ward held his curiosity about the dog in check until he saw Shannon lightly petting him with soft, tender strokes. Then he asked with his usual smile, "Where did the pup come from?"

She told him about Kenny looking for Pokey last evening. "Somehow Pokey made his way to my cottage, and I put him in the back seat. I'd only driven a short distance when all of a sudden he jumped into the front seat and startled me." Her voice faltered.

He could guess the rest of the story. She'd inadvertently turned the steering wheel, and the car dropped off the road.

"It was stupid," she said in a tone that was edged with disgust for herself.

He was surprised she'd bothered with the dog in the first place. He suspected that underneath that polished exterior of hers, there might be a deep, caring nature.

"Things like that happen to everyone," he assured her.

"Not to me," she said firmly. "I should have made sure that the dog stayed in the back."

"Well, no harm done," he said.

Her eyes rounded as she stared at him. "How can you say that? No harm done? My car will probably end up smashed to smithereens and my belongings burned to a crisp."

"True. I guess it's just the way you look at it. Since you escaped without being smashed to smithereens and burned with the rest of it, I'd say no real harm was done." He shot her a quick glance. Didn't she realize how blessed she was that she'd run off the road in that exact spot? There were a hundred other places where there were no rock ledges to halt a sheer drop into the canyon below. "It's all a matter of perspective, isn't it?"

Shannon tightened her jaw and didn't answer. What she didn't need was someone reminding her that she should be grateful instead of resentful about the whole thing. If he started lecturing her about families who had lost everything, she silently vowed she'd get out and walk.

Ward knew she was shaken up and still scared by what had happened. He could appreciate the toll the experience had taken on her nerves, because his own were still on edge from the ordeal. Even now he could feel sweat beading on the back of his neck if he thought about what could have happened.

They drove in silence until they reached the school parking lot. As soon as Ward turned off the engine, a man with a clipboard came over to the pickup's window.

"Is she the one not accounted for?" he asked Ward as he shot a quick look at Shannon.

"Yes. She had a little accident that delayed her."

The man grunted as if he thought one feeble excuse was as good as another. "The wind is kicking up. They've called in some more tankers. Hot flames could crest the ridge by nightfall."

"Or the fire could burn back on itself," Ward countered, believing that positive and negative thoughts created their own energy.

"Well, you're about the only one who thinks so," the man said flatly and walked away.

Shannon swallowed hard. How much time left before the whole mountain went up in flames? "What are the chances of getting a wrecker to pull my car back on the road?"

"Under normal conditions, Ed's Towing Service could give it a try. If the car stays hung up on those rocks, a pulley and cable could probably bring it up without too much trouble."

She felt a spurt of hope. "So if they put out the fire before it reaches the ridge, and it's safe to go back up the mountain, they could do it pretty fast?"

"Yes, they could—under normal conditions." He hated to douse the sudden spark in her lovely wide eyes as he added, "But I'm afraid as long as the whole area is in a fire zone and restricted to official personnel, the car will have to stay where it is."

"I see." She turned away so he couldn't see her face. Above everything else, she wasn't going to give into any feminine weakness that would add to her humiliation.

Shannon clutched the small dog in her arms as they made their way into the gym, and she searched the crowd for a glimpse of Kenny. Putting Pokey into the child's arms was suddenly more important than anything else.

Kenny saw her before she saw him. His childish cry of joy was unmistakable as he bounded across the floor. "You found Pokey."

"Here he is. Safe and sound." She smiled as she set the dog down, and Kenny fell on his knees, giggling as the pup washed his face with kisses.

"I love you, Pokey," he blubbered. "Where were you? I couldn't find you anywhere."

Shannon's eyes were suddenly misty as she saw the joyful reunion. She wasn't aware that Ward's hand had slipped into hers until she realized she was squeezing it. When she looked at him, she saw a warmth in his eyes that took her completely by surprise. Her defenses against allowing anyone to come too close emotionally shot into play, and she quickly withdrew her hand.

"She found Pokey. She found Pokey," Kenny shouted to everyone.

All Shannon's efforts to stay removed from everyone's notice were wiped out in that happy moment. She felt horribly on display as Alice Gordon loudly thanked her over and over again, and other people, young and old, gathered around her, smiling broadly.

Laura Cozzins's round face beamed at Shannon. "Bless you. That little tyke has been pining away for his dog. It's a good deed you've done this day."

"You don't know what that good deed cost her. Maybe Shannon will tell you about it sometime," Ward said. His smile wavered. "Then again, maybe she won't. She's a very private person," he added, smarting a little at the way she had quickly dropped his hand.

Laura nodded in a knowing way. As a minister's wife, she was obviously adept at reading emotions that lay beneath the surface. "How about a glass of lemonade and maybe a doughnut to refresh the two of you?" she suggested as if she were dedicated to feeding the body, as well as the soul at every opportunity.

"Thanks, but I've promised to deliver some supplies to the base camp," Ward said, "I'm already late by a couple of hours."

Shannon silently winced. They both knew it was her fault he'd been delayed. She quickly took her overnight bag from him and apologized, "I'm sorry I held you up. Thank you for...for everything."

"Rescuing damsels in distress is one of my special talents," he assured her solemnly as his eyes twinkled at her, and his mouth eased into a soft smile. "Call on me anytime."

She wanted to say something lightly back, but she couldn't. Her heart was too heavy.

"It's going to be okay." He gave her shoulder a light squeeze. Ward wanted to suggest that she join the others in prayer and meditation. Maybe, instead of shutting out God, she would gain assurance that she wasn't ever alone, no matter what the circumstances. He'd come to his faith the hard way, and he knew Shannon was on the same kind of path. "I'll try to come back this evening before I head to the ranch."

She watched as his broad back and muscular body disappeared out the door. Laura had been watching the exchange between them. With a knowing smile, she slipped her arm through Shannon's. "Come on, you can help me make some sandwiches for lunch."

The day was long and trying, and only the hope that Ward would come back kept Shannon's spirits from scraping bottom. The danger of firefighting became personal when Laura told her a story about a teenage Ward trying to handle a meadow fire all by himself and nearly getting trapped by the blaze before help got there.

Her heart contracted with a sudden jolt. Surely, Ward had enough sense to leave the fighting to the professionals. He was just delivering supplies, she reassured herself, but how well she knew that he wouldn't think of his safety in a time of danger.

All afternoon and evening, she kept an eye out for him, but he didn't show. It was Ted who came in late that evening and told her Ward had already gone to the ranch.

She wasn't surprised. No doubt he'd had enough of her trauma and drama. Remembering the way she had gone into his arms and accepted his tender caresses, she chided herself for letting her emotions play her for a fool. As she lay stiffly on her sagging cot, she firmly resolved she wouldn't make that mistake again. She knew better than to give her emotions free rein. There was always a price to pay for letting anyone too close. She had plenty of scars to prove it.

Chapter Three

Shannon slept very little that night. About two o'clock in the morning, fifty firefighters from a unit in Idaho arrived at the school. Since it was too late to make it to the base camp, they crowded into the gym with the rest of the refugees.

Shannon was up early and helped serve breakfast. Being in the midst of these brave young people who were willing to put their lives in danger was a startling revelation to her. Many times she had watched television coverage of California wildfires or heard about some fighter losing his or her life, but she had only been touched on a superficial level. Now that detachment disappeared, and her heart was filled with personal concern as she moved among these dedicated men who were going to battle a fierce, monstrous wildfire that was out of control.

When Reverend Cozzins said a prayer for their safety, Shannon bowed her head with everyone else and murmured a fervent amen. Even though she wanted to believe in some kind of heavenly protection, she knew it would take a faith stronger than hers to rely on any divine miracles.

The crew of firefighters left the school right after breakfast, leaving behind a mounting tension and anxiety in the crowded school. A briefing bulletin posted on the bulletin board later that morning was not encouraging. The prediction was for strong winds and high temperatures. Numerous infrared photos taken of the fire's boundary showed an ever widening area of destruction.

"We have to do something to keep the children occupied," declared Laura. In her usual energetic manner, she immediately started enlisting help to get some activities going. She organized several groups to play some outdoor games on the school grounds and sent some of the youngest children into the library to listen to stories.

Shannon had no intention of volunteering for anything or calling attention to herself in any way, but Kenny had different ideas. With childish pride, he pointed her out to all the kids.

"She's the one who found Pokey. He was lost, and the fire almost got him. But she saved him, didn't you, Shannon?"

The cluster of grinning children beamed at Shannon in a way that made her want to sink into the floor. What could she say without taking away Kenny's moment in the limelight? "I didn't exactly find him—he found me."

Laura Cozzins suddenly appeared at Shannon's side, saving her from having to say anything more about Kenny's dog. "Well, now, I see you've already made friends with Kenny and his pals. Wonderful, Shannon." She beamed. "Why don't you take them into the art room and let them draw and color and make all kinds of wonderful things?" She smiled broadly as she elicited nodding approval from the kids. "Doesn't that sound like fun, children?"

Shannon could have summoned a hundred reasons why she was the last person in the world to be put in charge of a bunch of kids, but she didn't have a chance.

Kenny grabbed her hand. "You can be our teacher."

The rest of children nodded and crowded around her with smiles and beaming faces, effectively eliminating any chance she had for refusal. As the children began to pull Shannon toward the classroom Laura completely ignored her frantic plea for help.

"You'll have fun," Laura promised with a chuckle, and quickly turned away to draft someone else for one of her projects.

How in the world did I get myself into this? Shannon would have rather faced a roomful of hostile executives than a roomful of squirrelly youngsters. Raised as an only child by parents who never stayed in one city very long, she had always been the new kid in school, and being around younger children had never been a part of her upbringing. She grew up in an adult world where achievement and success were the driving goals. As a result, Shannon was competitive, motivated and competent when it came to the business world, but it only took ten minutes in the art classroom with a cluster of scattering children to discover that her people-management skills were sadly lacking in the present situation.

"Everyone sit down," she said in a normal voice, which had little impact in the noise level of excited kids darting about the room, handling everything that wasn't tacked or glued down.

Boxes of donated supplies were on the tables. She knew that if she didn't do something, impatient children would be diving into them, and the chaos would grow worse by the minute. It didn't help her confidence to realize no one in the room was paying any attention to her.

She had to take charge, and quickly. Remembering that one of the first rules of a successful business leader was to command attention, she clapped her hands loudly and raised her voice above the bedlam. "Listen to me! I want everyone to sit down now! And be quiet!"

Later Shannon wondered what she would have done if the kids had ignored her, but to her relief, they quickly filled the chairs at two long tables and fixed their grinning smiles on her. She guessed that their ages ranged from kindergarten to second or third grades. Now that she had their attention she didn't know what to do with it.

She walked over to a table and looked at the boxes of pencils, crayons, paper and a few coloring books. She cleared her throat, hoping she would sound steadier than she felt. "All right, we're going to draw and color pictures."

"I want a picture to color," a curly-headed girl

named Heather howled when Shannon gave the last coloring book page to someone else.

"I bet you can draw a nice picture of your own to color," Shannon coaxed.

Heather set her lips in a pugnacious line. "I want a real picture."

"Sorry. I'm afraid that there aren't any coloring book pictures left," Shannon said flatly.

"Then you draw me one," Heather ordered with pouting lips, and shoved her plain sheet of paper toward Shannon.

Fuming silently, Shannon grabbed a pencil, and as quickly as she could she sketched a house with a flower garden and tall tree with a child's swing in it. "There. Color that."

Heather looked at it, then gave Shannon a broad smile of approval. "It's nice."

"I'm glad you like it," Shannon said in relief as the little girl picked out some crayons and began to color the picture.

Shannon dropped down in the teacher's chair and wondered how long it would be before she could send all the kids back to the gym.

When Heather finished coloring her picture, she started showing everyone and bragging, "See the picture teacher drew for me."

"I want one, too." The children began to line up at her desk, all of them wanting a special picture of their own. "Draw me something, teacher."

Shannon's first reaction was to refuse, but somewhere at the back of her memory was a remembered pleasure in what her parents had called her doodling.

Even though an art teacher had told Shannon once that she had an artistic flair, she'd had never had time or the inclination to foster it. Giving a soft laugh, she said, "All right, let's see what I can do."

Quickly she sketched some simple scenes, then some cartoon figures that seemed to come easily to her. As she handed each drawing to a child, she was rewarded with a broad grin and a thank-you.

"Do one for me," Kenny begged.

"Well, let's see." Shannon pretended to think. "I bet I know one you'd like."

She was drawing a cute puppy with ears and a tail just like Pokey when she was startled by someone leaning over her shoulder. "Very good," Ward said, as his warm breath bathed her ear.

Startled and instantly embarrassed, Shannon almost covered the sketch of the puppy with her hand so he couldn't see. A deep conditioning from her childhood had made her instinctively want to hide what she had been doing. She could almost hear her father's voice. *Wasting your time again, Shannon!*

As Ward saw the muscles in Shannon's cheek tighten, he reassured her. "I mean it. It's very good."

"It's Pokey," Kenny said happily. "I'm going to color him black and white. And I'll stay in the lines," he promised solemnly, as if someone had pointed out this little goal to him once or twice. He proudly took the picture to his table.

Ward eased down on the corner of her desk, lightly swinging one leg as he looked around the room. "I didn't know you were a teacher in the making."

"I'm not."

"You could have fooled me."

He grinned at her, and she didn't know if he was secretly amused or impressed that the children weren't climbing the walls.

"What brings you back to the school this morning?" she asked lightly. She wasn't going to let him know that she'd been disappointed when he hadn't come to the school at all yesterday.

"I had a little time between chores and helping out the fire wardens this afternoon. When I came in, Laura asked me to deliver a message to you."

"And what was that?" Shannon stiffened, wondering if the preacher's wife had come up with another volunteer job for her.

"It's time to let the kids go to lunch."

She looked at her watch in surprise It was almost noon. She couldn't believe the morning had passed so quickly. When she announced that it was time for lunch, there were some protests from those who wanted to finish their pictures.

Shannon vaguely promised they could finish their pictures some other time or take them with them. Ward sat on the edge of the desk watching Shannon while she collected crayons, pencils and paper. For some reason, his smiling approval was irritating.

"Well?" she demanded, challenging him to say something. "You don't have to look so smug. Laura caught me at a time when I had no chance to refuse."

"It looks like she drafted the right person, all right."

"At least it's better than peeling potatoes, thank you."

* * *

Ward laughed, secretly relieved to find her spitting words at him instead of curled up somewhere battling fear. He had some bad news for her. Flying sparks carried by the wind had ignited the tops of tall ponderosa pines on the other side of the high-ridge fire line. Ground crews were scrambling to clear brush in the area, and airplane tankers were dropping fire retardant chemicals in an effort to control the blaze before it became full-blown and started down the mountainside. A dozen homes were in danger of being lost—as well as a white sports car still perched precariously on a rugged rocky slope.

"What is it?" Shannon asked as his smile faded and his forehead furrowed in a frown. Her hands tightened on the piece of paper she was holding, crushing it. "My car's gone, isn't it?"

"No, it's still there."

"But?" she prodded.

"The fire is threatening to start down this side of the mountain. New fire lines are being set up, and crews are cutting down brush and trees around some of the high mountain homes in an effort to save them."

"And if they don't stop it?" Even as she asked, she knew the answer.

"It could sweep down the mountain to the river and spread along the valley below." He didn't add that his ranch would be vulnerable to any fire sweeping up the canyon toward his pastureland. "We're all praying that that doesn't happen. Which reminds me, we're going to have church services here at the school on Sunday. Our little church won't hold this crowd, and I'm sure there'll be a lot more worshipers than usual." He gave her a wry smile. "Lots of people wait to make a 911 call to the Lord, you know, instead of keeping prayed up."

Shannon refrained from commenting. She hadn't seen any evidence that churchgoing people had it any easier in life than anybody else. The only time she was ever in a church was for weddings and her parents' funeral. Neither her mother nor her father had held to any religious faith, and she had been brought up to believe that being a "good" person was all that was necessary.

Ward could tell from her expression that worship was not a part of her life, and for some reason, he felt challenged by her lack of spiritual awareness.

"What do you say to lunch at Bette's Diner?" he asked impulsively. "It's only a short walk from here, and I bet getting out of here for even an hour would do you good."

Shannon searched his face. Was it pity that prompted the invitation? Or did he need an hour away from the heavy pressures as much as she did? There were shadows under his dark-brown eyes and visible lines in his forehead and around his mouth. She wondered how much sleep he was getting these nights.

"Sounds great," she said honestly.

As they left the school, they passed a roped-off area where anxious pet owners were milling around kennels and cages lined up by the building. Shannon couldn't believe the menagerie of animals—cats, rabbits, dogs and other furry creatures—that had been brought to the school for safekeeping. When Shannon spied Kenny running across the playground with Pokey on a leash, she waved and smiled at him.

"You ought to do that more often," Ward told her.

"Do what?"

"Smile instead of frown."

"Oh, is that your way of saying I look like a sour-puss?"

"Yep."

They both laughed, and he took her hand with a playful swing. As his long fingers gently closed around hers, she felt a kind of peace and harmony that denied the biting odor of smoke and the wailing of emergency vehicles.

Neither spoke as they walked slowly away from the school. Shannon was surprised at her sudden sense of freedom from the pressures that had been weighing her down. Nothing had changed. Nothing at all. Her life was still in the pits, but somehow, walking hand-in-hand with him, she felt in a world apart from the shambles of her life. She'd never allowed her feelings to dominate her rational thoughts before, and every ounce of common sense told her to shut down this emotional reaction before she lost her mind completely, but she kept her hand in his, drawing warmth and reassurance from the touch.

They strolled down the hill until they reached Main Street—two blocks of clustered rustic buildings that housed one gas station, a small mercantile store, a feed store, several small businesses and one restaurant named Bette's Diner.

Schoolchildren were bused into Beaver Junction from the whole county, since most of the population lived on ranches and scattered mountain homes. At the moment, the influx of outsiders was ten times the normal population, and the tiny network of roads around the Junction was snarled with emergency vehicles.

Bette's Diner was crowded from one end to the other, and Ward and Shannon were lucky to squeeze into a booth just as a couple of men vacated it. They didn't have to wait long for service. They had barely seated themselves when a waitress breezed over to them with a welcoming smile aimed at Ward.

"Hi, there. I was wondering if you were going to make it for lunch today. Somebody told me you were up at the base camp shortly after dawn."

Shannon recognized the attractive brunette who had hugged and laughed with Ward in the gym that first afternoon. She was still dressed in Western pants and shirt, and a small apron encircled her waist. Shannon guessed she was probably in her late twenties, and the way her eyes lit on Ward made it easy to tell how she felt about the rancher.

"Judy, this is Shannon Hensley," Ward said, quickly introducing her. "She's waiting out the fire at the school."

"Yes, I know," Judy said as she darted a quick glance at Shannon. "From Hollywood, someone told me. Of course, you can't believe everything you hear."

"It's true. Would you like her autograph?" Ward asked with mock solemnity.

"Are you...somebody?" Judy's eyes widened as she stared at Shannon.

"Of course, she is. Would I bring a nobody to Bette's Diner for lunch?" Ward asked facetiously.

"Don't pay any attention to him," Shannon said with a laugh. "I'm a working girl from Los Angeles." And out of a job, she could have added.

A faint color rose in Judy's cheeks. "I should know better than to fall for his joshing." As she readied her pad and pencil for their order, she became all business. "What can I bring you?"

Shannon followed Ward's suggestion and ordered baked trout, which he promised was caught fresh daily. After Judy disappeared into the kitchen with their orders, Shannon chided Ward, "Shame on you. You shouldn't tease her like that. She likes you."

"I know, but humor is the best defense for a lot of things, like letting friendship get out of hand."

The way he said it made Shannon wonder if he kept all the women at arm's length. And she remembered what Laura Cozzins had told her.

"Well, what's your verdict?" he asked with a raised eyebrow as he leaned back in the booth.

"What do you mean?"

"I'll tell you a little secret. Your eyes deepen into a startling gray-blue when you're doing some heavy thinking." His smile challenged her. "Now, don't lie and tell me you were thinking about what kind of pie to order for dessert."

"All right," she said, resting her elbows on the table. "I was indulging in curiosity about some things Laura shared with me."

He chuckled. "Well, then, I suppose I should start to deny everything just on principle."

"Oh, she was very complimentary. She bragged about your ranch and explained that you specialize in raising Appaloosa horses. Frankly, I have no idea what makes one horse different from any other horse.''

"A real city slicker, eh? Well, you've come to the right place to get a little equine education.'' There was an unmistakable lift of happiness to his voice as he began to tell her about his stable of Appaloosa horses. "They have beautiful markings. Brown and black spots, with white or black tails and mane, are the most common coloring. A wonderful saddle horse, and one of the best mounts for working cattle. The best thing that ever happened to me was coming back to the ranch to devote myself to raising and breeding them.''

"What were you doing with your life before that?''

"Nothing I'm proud of,'' his said flatly. "My daughter was only two when my wife died, so I decided to move back to the homestead so my sister could raise her. You'll have to come out to the ranch and meet them.''

"I'm really hoping to get out of here the first chance I get,'' she responded quickly. For some reason, she didn't want to commit herself to any personal involvement with his family. It was enough of a strain to try to adjust to a bunch of strangers. The less she knew about anyone, especially this very attractive man, the easier it would be to maintain her distance and not get emotionally involved. What a mistake it had been coming to Colorado in the first place. She'd been running away, she could admit that now. Afraid and scared, she'd thought of a mountain cottage as a sanctuary. What a laugh that was!

Ward didn't know why the barriers had gone up. Probably she was bored to tears with all his horse talk.

He wondered why he was so intent upon impressing her. Anyone with a lick of sense could see that his lackluster life wouldn't hold any charm for her. They were from different worlds, and only a crisis like this fire would have put the two of them together in the first place. It bothered him that he couldn't figure her out. Spoiled? Certainly. Vain? Probably. Hurting? Definitely.

When Judy served their orders, she made light conversation with Ward and then lowered her voice in a personal tone. "Am I going to see you tonight?"

"Afraid not," Ward answered readily, giving her his easy smile. "Chores at the ranch have gotten ahead of me. I have to head back as early this afternoon as I can."

Judy looked ready to protest and shot a quick look at Shannon as she turned away.

Was he breaking a date with her, Shannon wondered. It was obvious that the waitress thought she was going to see him tonight. Were they more than just friends? If Judy was his sweetheart, Shannon didn't approve of the way he might be standing her up. Was this his usual way of toying with the opposite sex? Her earlier warm and comfortable feeling about him was gone. They finished their meal with only sporadic, desultory conversation.

As they came out of the café, Shannon decided she wanted to pick up a few things at the mercantile store. "I'd like to buy some more coloring books. I don't want a repeat of this morning."

"Why not? I'd say you are really talented, drawing all those pictures. Are you an artist in the making?"

"Me?" Shannon protested quickly. "Heavens, no. That's just doodling—at least that's what my mother called it. She used to get furious with me for wasting my time, drawing pictures all over my notebooks and scratch pads. Believe me, I haven't done anything like that for years."

"That's too bad. You looked as if you were enjoying it."

"I was just relieved to find something that would keep the children quiet. It's worth buying some coloring books to keep them busy."

There was a crowd in the small, old-fashioned store. Long counters were piled high with a variety of merchandise, and Isabel Watkins and another clerk were kept busy waiting on the customers. Shannon and Ward went their separate ways for a few minutes, and she found a half dozen coloring books, which could be torn apart. She also purchased several children's card games, which she intended to donate to Laura's recreational activities.

Ward was waiting at the checkout counter with a small sack of his own when she finished shopping. If another day or two went by without her belongings, she knew she'd have to spend some money to replace a good many things. As it was, she was already over the weekly budget she'd set for herself.

"Would you mind waiting while I make a telephone call?" she asked Ward when she spied a phone booth a short distance down the street. The telephone number she'd given the employment agency was useless—she had packed her cell phone in her cosmetic case when her purse had been too full to hold it. "It'll just take a moment."

"Sure thing." He took all the sacks and leaned against the corner of the booth as she closed the door and made her call. It didn't take long to hear the same disappointing story. No response on her résumés yet.

"Keep in touch," the artificial, upbeat voice of the employment lady told her.

Ward refrained from asking any questions as they walked in silence to the school, but he could tell from the flickering tightness in the muscles around her mouth that the telephone call had not been a happy one.

Reverend Cozzins was coming out of the door of the school when they reached it. The minister was as tall and gangly as his wife was short and rounded, but both exuded the same small-town friendliness. "Ward, will we see you at the church meeting tonight?"

"Sorry, Reverend." Ward shook his head. "It's like I told Judy. I've got to catch up on my chores. Just sign me up for whatever needs doing, and I'll try to squeeze it in."

So he didn't have a romantic date with Judy. Shannon didn't know what she felt, but it seemed to be an undefinable sense of satisfaction.

"You're a good man." Paul Cozzins gave Ward a healthy pat on the shoulder. Then he smiled at Shannon. "My wife tells me you did a great job with the children this morning. Some of the kids were so proud of the pictures you drew for them that they posted them on one of the bulletin boards."

"What?" stammered Shannon. "You have to be kidding."

He smiled and shook his head.

"But I didn't draw them for display."

"You've got a God-given talent, young lady. No need to be hiding it."

Ward chuckled. "Some people seek glory and others have glory thrust upon them," he quoted, his eyes twinkling.

Cozzins looked at a piece of paper he held in his hand. "Well, now. I'd best get along. That woman of mine gave me a foot-long list of things to do. See you later." With a wave of his hand, he hurried off.

Shannon saw Ward's mouth quirking with a grin, and she warned him, "Don't you dare laugh. It's not funny. You don't know how horrified my mother would be to have my doodling exhibited like that for all to see."

"Are you sure? I don't see how giving pleasure to other people could upset anyone. Of course, if you want to insist, I'm sure the kids will take their colored drawings down."

"You know I can't do that."

He nodded, smiling smugly. "Yep."

She quickly put on her protective armor of pretend indifference as they went into the school. "It isn't as if anyone really knows me. I guess there's no harm done."

Ward carried her things to her cot in one corner of the gym. "I probably won't be back for a day or two. We have to move some horses into a far pasture, because they get antsy when they smell the thickening smoke haze even though it's miles away, thank God."

She tried to hide her disappointment. His company was the only bright spot in a long, boring day. "Thanks for lunch," she managed. "And the chance to do a little shopping. Oh, this sack is yours," she said, picking up the bag he'd laid on her cot.

"No, it isn't. It's something especially for you."

Before she could respond, he turned and disappeared in a crowd moving out the front door. Slowly she opened the sack and peered inside.

What in the—

With an uncertain laugh that had an edge of tears in it, she pulled out the contents—an artist's drawing pad and a box of colored pencils. She couldn't believe how special this simple gift made her feel. It honored a part of herself that she'd tried to keep hidden. For the first time, she held the drawing pencils with a sense of excitement and delight.

Chapter Four

The next morning, Shannon gathered with the other refugees in the gym to hear the latest update on the situation. Despite the call for more and more firefighters and equipment, the wildfire kept spreading like the tentacles of a greedy octopus. It consumed the southern side of the mountain where it had started, but the good news was that the blaze hadn't crowned any of the tall trees on Prospect Ridge. If the fire burned itself out before cresting the ridge, scattered mountain homes and Shannon's car on the northern side would be saved.

A hopeful murmur ran through the crowded school. "Maybe we'll be getting back into our homes soon, after all."

And maybe I can get someone to pull my car back onto the road, Shannon silently added, suddenly filled with hope that there might be a quick end to this nightmare. She was clinging to this optimistic possibility when her morning walk took her around the school, where she spied a tow truck in the parking lot. The painted sign on the side read Pete's Gas Station, and a husky, middle-aged man was busy hooking an old station wagon to a cable.

Shannon remembered Ward saying something about the possibility that a tow truck might be able to pull her car on the road. Hope sprang like a geyser as she hurried to the tow truck.

"Pardon me," she said to the man who was bent over the front of the station wagon. Either he didn't hear her, or he was concentrating too hard on fastening the tow chain to pay any attention to her.

She waited impatiently for a moment, then raised her voice. "Pardon me, I'm sorry to interrupt you, but I want to talk to you about towing my car."

He finished locking a cable before straightening up.

"Just point it out," he said as he looked around the parking lot. "Which one is it?"

"Oh, it's not here." She searched for an explanation that would best explain the situation, and at the back of her mind was a nagging concern about how much he would charge. "I'm afraid I had a little accident." She turned and pointed. "It's on the side of that mountain. About halfway down, I think. It got hung up on some rocks and—"

"Oh, you're the one." His mouth spread in a broad, tobacco-stained grin. "The city gal."

Shannon could feel heat surging to her face. Did everyone know about her mishap? The way the man was grinning made it plain she'd been the topic of some belly laughs. No doubt she had been the butt of a lot of jokes about California drivers.

"Yes, I'm the city gal," Shannon admitted, forcing a smile. Somehow, she knew this was not the time to demand service in a brisk, businesslike way. "Apparently you've heard about my little accident."

"Yep, Ward Dawson was in the station, talking to me about it." Peering at her from under his bushy eyebrows, he said, "He was saying that you must have had an angel riding with you, for sure."

"He already asked you to take care of it?" Shannon didn't know whether she was pleased or irritated. "He didn't say a word to me about it."

"Ward knows that Pete Shornberger is darn good at pulling cars back on the road," he bragged, chewing on a toothpick as he talked. "Ward's family and mine go way back. He's one fine fellow. We all missed the guy when he went off for a few years. We're mighty glad he's back—to stay." He gave her a brisk nod. "This is where he belongs."

Was there a warning in his tone? It was almost as if somebody had been trying to make something out of the time she and Ward had spent together. She bristled. Small-town gossip had already probably cast her in the role of a big-city man catcher. "He certainly has been helpful to everyone," Shannon said with a deliberate emphasis on the *everyone*.

"Ward's a good man. His mom and pa were good Christian folks. They'd be proud of the way Ward and his sister turned out." He said it in a tone that made her think he'd already heard she hadn't joined any of the prayer groups or lined up with any of the church folk.

"Well, I'm glad he has already talked to you about

recovering the car as soon as possible," she said, side-stepping any personal observations about Ward.

"Yep, as soon as the road is open, we'll give it a try—if the car's still there." The way he said it, Shannon knew he fully expected the car to be at the bottom of the canyon by then.

"This morning's report on the fire looked good. Maybe they'd let you get at it sometime today," she said hopefully.

He took the toothpick out of his mouth and threw it away. Without commenting on her suggestion, he climbed into his truck and towed the station wagon out of the parking lot.

Dispirited, Shannon went into the building, and once again, Laura asked her to take the same group of children into the art room.

"Isn't there someone else?" she begged. Every time she passed the large bulletin board where the children had posted all the pictures she had drawn for them, she experienced a mixture of feelings. Her sketches were as good as those in the coloring books. In fact, some of them were better because they contained more detail, she admitted secretly. And her cartoon figures had a happy, whimsical air to them that surprised her.

"You have a God-given talent, Shannon. Why are you afraid to use it?"

"I'm not afraid," she protested. "It's just that I haven't had any reason to spend time that way—"

"Until now," Laura finished for her.

Shannon didn't know how she could argue that she didn't have time for such "doodling." There were no telephones ringing, no meetings to attend, no baskets of reports to fill out. All she had at the moment was time.

She gave Laura a surrendering smile. ''All right, I'll go draw pictures.''

As she sketched pictures for the children to color, a remembered joy in drawing came back, and she began to think about making some sketches for her own pleasure. She knew that Ward would be pleased if she made use of the drawing pad and pencils he'd given her.

Later she moved quietly around the gym, careful not to draw attention to herself as she sought to catch in pencil drawings the essence of some of the things around her. At first the pencils felt awkward in her hand, but she couldn't believe how soon the harmony of her eye and hand began to create a variety of shaded figures and simple backgrounds. Long-forgotten compliments from her school art teachers came back as she instinctively responded to the need for balance and perspective.

She sketched an old man sitting in a rocking chair, reading his Bible. As the drawing took shape, she couldn't help but wonder how many things he'd left behind to make room to bring that old chair.

In another corner of the school, a circle of older women was busily doing handwork as if they belonged to some impromptu sewing bee. She didn't try to do portraits but sought to catch the essence, expressions and body forms of the individuals she was sketching.

Her best effort was a young mother holding a sleeping baby while another child played at her feet, and she was startled when a young man approached her. As he glanced quickly at the sketch pad in her hand, she quickly closed it, instantly guarded. It was almost as if someone had caught her doodling—again.

"I don't mean to intrude," he said quickly. "I'm Kenny's father, Tom, and I want to thank you for rescuing his dog the way you did."

"Oh," she said, feeling foolish because she'd let his casual glance at the drawing pad make her feel defensive. Kenny had inherited the same thatch of blond hair and sun-freckled face as his father.

"It's nice to meet you," she said, holding out her hand. "You have a wonderful little boy."

"He thinks you're pretty special, too. He never gets tired of telling everyone how Miss Shannon saved Pokey." Tom Gordon hesitated. "I hope you won't think me too forward, but I saw you sketching my wife's grandfather. I wonder if you'd let me see it. I know you're a talented artist—"

Shannon's mouth fell open, and she couldn't hold back a laugh. "I'm not an artist. Far from it."

He shook his head. "Call it what you will, the kids are crazy about the pictures you draw for them to color."

"And that's about the height and breadth of my talent. I'm just amusing myself by making some simple line drawings. The sketch I made of your wife's grandfather is an impression of an old man sitting in a rocking chair, reading a Bible. It's not any kind of portrait."

"May I see it?"

Even as a deep instinct to flatly refuse him flared, a warning was also there that she'd come off as some ridiculous temperamental adolescent if she refused. She didn't want the small community to have any more ammunition for their talk about the city woman.

"All right." She quickly flipped open the drawing pad. "See, it's just a sketch of no one in particular. It's not Kenny's grandfather or anyone else."

"But it could be," he said thoughtfully. "It could be."

The way he said it was like a healing balm to her spirit. None of her professional achievements had given her more satisfaction than she felt at the moment. She couldn't believe how much peace and joy flooded through her, and when he asked if he could have it, she readily removed the sketch from the drawing pad and gave it to him.

A whole day passed without any sign of Ward. Even though he had warned her that he would be working at the ranch, her eyes still kept roving around the crowded gym, hoping to see him.

In the early evening, she took several walks around the school, searching for a glimpse of his pickup. Maybe, just maybe, she would spy his reddish-brown hair and broad shoulders moving toward her with that winning grin of his, but night came and there was no sign of him.

Shannon was irritated with herself for indulging in such adolescent behavior, and when Laura asked her if she'd seen Ward, she answered vaguely, "No, I don't believe I have."

"Well, I'm sure he'll be here tomorrow," Laura said with a knowing nod of her gray head.

"I wouldn't plan on it," Shannon answered, surprised at the crispness of her tone. She knew then that she was speaking as much to herself as to the reverend's wife.

"Oh? Why not?"

"He'll probably be working," Shannon said vaguely. "I think he said he had to catch up on chores at the ranch."

"But tomorrow's Sunday," Laura protested, as if she couldn't believe Shannon had forgotten. "He knows we're holding church service here, and I don't think chores are going to keep him from honoring the Lord's day. When his wife died and Ward brought his little daughter back home to raise, he decided to put God first in his life. I can't imagine anything or anyone strong enough to make him ignore the Sabbath."

Shannon fell silent because she didn't know what the proper response should be. Maybe it was her imagination, but she had the impression there seemed to be a subtle warning in Laura's words. Surely the woman didn't think it would be Shannon's fault if Ward didn't show up for Sunday services. Shannon silently fumed. Were people jumping to a lot of stupid conclusions about her pairing up with Ward just because they'd spent a little time together?

"You'll join us, of course," Laura said as if there wasn't any question about Shannon ignoring worship services.

The next morning, Shannon changed her mind a dozen times about whether or not she would go into the small auditorium with the others. As the time came for services to start, the gym emptied, and she was one

of a few remaining behind. In spite of herself, she kept
an eye on the front door, but there was no sign of
Ward. Apparently the preacher's wife was wrong about
his dedication to attending church services.

Disappointed, she finally wandered down the hall to
the auditorium and sat in the back row where there
were a few vacant seats. She didn't know the hymn
they were singing, and there were no hymnals, but most
of the gathering seemed to know the song. It was a
rollicking song about a little church in the wildwood,
which Shannon thought was a strange selection for this
makeshift worship service in a school gym. She didn't
understand the joyful lilt in their voices and the relaxed
expressions on their faces. When a deep masculine
voice joined in, she turned her head with a start.

"No place is so dear to my childhood," Ward sang
as he slipped into a seat beside her and finished the
lyrics to the song. Then he leaned over and whispered,
"Thanks for saving me a place."

Her first impulse was to protest that she wasn't even
thinking about him, but it didn't seem the right time or
place to lie. A masculine, spicy scent from his morning
shave teased her nostrils, and his crisply ironed shirt
and newly creased pants had a fresh scent of their own.
All her senses seemed to vibrate with the awareness of
his presence. Sitting beside him, listening to his deep,
resonant voice as he repeated prayers and sang with
great feeling, she felt like an intruder and a fraud.

The worship service poured over Shannon, making
only a ripple in her consciousness. She wasn't familiar
with any of the scripture readings or the selections sung
by the small choir. Reverend Cozzins's message left

her unmoved. Surrounded by people who had lost their homes or were in danger of everything they had going up in smoke at any hour, it seemed utter folly for any of them to believe that "All things work to the good to those who love the Lord."

How could any good or blessing come out of this devastating situation? She didn't want to challenge what anyone believed, but as far as she was concerned, trying to justify everything as God's will was totally illogical.

She envied Ward's tranquillity, his worshipful, peaceful demeanor as he closed his eyes, bowed his head and let his large hands rest quietly on his lap. In spite of the physical and emotional demands that had been made upon him since the fire began, he never seemed to lose his easygoing, confident manner.

When the service was over, Laura Cozzins bustled up to them as they were leaving the auditorium. "I saw you sneaking in." She teased Ward with a broad smile.

"Sorry, I was late. It took me a little longer to get chores done this morning because Ted spent the night at his grandmother's place. He wants to be ready to evacuate her if the fire heads down that canyon."

"Oh, my goodness. Is Rachel's place in danger?"

Ward nodded. "He would like to move her now before there's an emergency, but she's a stubborn old gal and won't budge."

"Where are Beth and Tara?" Laura Cozzins frowned. "I was hoping to talk to your sister this morning. She's such a help organizing everything, and we've got plenty of challenges ahead of us."

"Beth insisted on my coming to church while she

and Tara stayed and kept an eye on Calico—that's Tara's mare, and she's about to foal any time. It's going to be Tara's colt to raise, so she's really been taking care of the mare. I think my little daughter may have the makings of a veterinarian.''

"She's a smart little thing. Have you met Tara?'' Laura asked Shannon.

"No, she hasn't,'' Ward said quickly. "And I was just about to remedy that by inviting her out to the ranch for Sunday dinner.'' He gave Shannon that easygoing, engaging smile of his. "How about it? Would a nice ride up the valley and a homecooked meal appeal to you?''

The invitation totally surprised her. If she'd had time to think about it, she probably could have come up with some sensible reasons for refusing. "I would love to escape for a few hours,'' she surprised herself by saying, and added with a smile, "I think my social calendar is free.''

Ward suspected that her acceptance of his invitation had more to do with getting away than an eagerness for his company, but he was still pleased. He liked having her sitting close beside him in the worn seat of his pickup truck, and he was eager to show off his beautiful horses.

The road they traveled was cupped on both sides by wooded mountain slopes and bordered by a rushing white foam creek. Ward drove with the ease of someone who knew every bump in the road, and Shannon was glad that their direction was leading them away from the threatening fire and the gray haze that had been floating over Beaver Junction.

She kept her window rolled down to enjoy the clean, spicy pine smell. When the road suddenly broke through heavy stands of tall evergreens and a beautiful mountain valley came into view, she caught her breath.

"It's beautiful, isn't it?" Ward said when he saw the rapture on her face. "I never tire of this valley, summer or winter. It's God's own masterpiece."

A rambling, two-story white house stood in the middle of a deep green meadow laced with log fences. A steep-roofed barn and a line of stables, shaded by a cluster of aspen trees, had been built a short distance behind the house.

"Here's home," he said with pride. As they passed under an arched sign, Dawson Ranch, Ward pointed out some beautiful spotted horses grazing in the various corrals. "Those are three-year-olds. Just about ready for sale."

The graceful horses slowly raised their heads at the sound of the truck. They were sleek and beautiful, and no two were alike in their various spotted patterns of deep mahogany, brown and black.

When Shannon saw the loving pride in Ward's eyes, she realized that the proud smile on his face spoke of a man content with his life. She couldn't help but wonder what it would feel like to really have a home. She couldn't begin to remember all the rented apartments and leased houses that had been in her past. With every promotion, she'd been moving up the housing scale and had really overextended herself when she bought her last luxurious apartment. Even before six months had passed, she'd had her eye on an oceanside condo.

"I grew up in that house," he told her. "My parents

moved in with my grandfather as soon as they were married, and my sister and I were raised here. Beth stayed here after our parents passed away. I went off to college and got married. As a single father, I decided to come back here to raise my little girl and follow my dream of breeding and training saddle horses.'' He smiled at her. ''And the rest is history, so they say.''

He drove the pickup to the back of the house and parked at the side of a small vegetable garden. Even before he stepped out of the car, the back screen door flew open, and a small girl with pigtails flying came running out.

''What is it, Tara?'' Ward hurriedly got out of the truck. ''Is Calico—''

''Nope.'' She shook her head. ''She's not doing anything. Just standing and eating. I keep telling her to hurry up, 'cause I want to see my colt.'' Her dark-brown eyes flew to Shannon, who was still sitting in the front seat. ''Who's she?''

''A friend.''

''Is she going to help Calico drop her colt?''

Shannon saw an amused quirking at the corner of his mouth. ''No, I think Calico is going to have to do that on her own.''

As Shannon stepped out of the car, Tara looked at her curiously, taking in her pale-pink slacks suit, floral scarf and laced white sandals. ''Where'd she come from?''

''California,'' Ward answered, a knowing grin on his face as he watched his daughter's expression change from curiosity to excitement.

"California. She's from Hollywood? Golly, gee, I never thought I'd meet anyone from Disneyland."

Ward laughed as he put an affectionate hand on Tara's brown head. "Say hello to Shannon. Maybe she can explain that California, Hollywood, Disneyland and Sea World are not all the same thing."

"Yes, they are," his little daughter said with a pugnacious lift of her freckled nose. "If we went there, we could see them all."

Shannon chuckled. "That's absolutely true. I think she's got you there, Ward." She winked at Tara. "We'll have to see if we can't educate your dad."

"Do you want to see my tree house?" Tara asked Shannon as if anxious to please.

"Not now, Tara," Ward said quickly. "We better check in with Beth. She'll have all our scalps if she has to wait dinner on us. Shannon will be here all afternoon, so there'll be time to show her around."

"Okay," Tara agreed happily.

Ward beamed proudly as his daughter led them with a kind of hopping skip to the house.

The large modern kitchen was filled with wonderful scents of baking. Shannon could see that dinner was ready. Roasted chicken, seasoned dressing, freshly picked peas and all the fixings for a salad.

"Beth, we're here," called Ward.

A muffled voice from the pantry answered, "In a minute."

"Aunt Beth said we couldn't eat in the kitchen. We have to eat in the dining room," Tara said solemnly as if this change was something worthy of notice. "And I'm supposed to mind my manners. I don't know why she's making such a fuss. We never eat in the dining room except Easter and Christmas.''

Shannon realized that Ward had been so sure she would accept his invitation his sister had gone to a lot of extra trouble on her account. What if she had refused? She didn't like the position he had put her in by assuming she would come with him. Even under the circumstances, her independence was important to her.

A tall, rather large woman with reddish-brown hair darker than Ward's emerged from the pantry with a couple of jars of homemade jelly in her hands. Her smile was broad and friendly. She quickly put down the jelly, brushed her hands on her faded jeans and held out one to Shannon.

"Hi, I'm Beth. So glad you could come to dinner. Shannon, is it?"

"Yes, thank you for the invitation."

"Shannon's from Hollywood," Tara said, grinning widely.

"Or there about," Ward added with a chuckle.

Beth laughed. "Tara has her own sense of geography. And it doesn't do any good to straighten her out. In some ways she's like someone else I know," she said, sending her brother an affectionate glance. "How are you making out at the evacuation center, Shannon?"

"As well as everyone else, I guess. It's not easy on anyone. But we're all hopeful that they'll get the fire out any time now and we can all get back to our normal lives."

Shannon was grateful when Beth changed the subject and herded them into a high-ceilinged dining room paneled in warm cherry tones and filled with dappled light slanting through lace-draped windows.

When all the food was on the table, they bowed their heads, and Ward gave thanks for all their blessings in a simple prayer of gratitude. His easy, relaxed manner was in harmony with the feeling of the house, Shannon thought, as she found herself relaxing for the first time in days. She discovered that the appetite she thought she'd lost was back. Beth beamed when she asked for seconds.

Tara chatted about the vigil they were keeping on Calico. She seemed to know a lot more about horses than most adults. It was easy to see that Ward was proud of her, and Shannon suspected they spent a lot of time together, talking, sharing and having fun.

This kind of father-daughter relationship was foreign to Shannon. There had been very little companionship with her father. Grades and achievement had been the icons of his approval, and he'd been too busy to pay much attention to her as a child or successful career woman. The sad truth was that she had missed him very little when he died.

"Can we take Shannon for a horseback ride this afternoon?" Tara asked after dinner was over and Beth was serving a deep-dish strawberry and rhubarb pie for dessert.

"I guess we could arrange that," Ward answered, nodding.

"I think I'm much too full to go horseback riding," Shannon answered smoothly. Riding a horse was certainly not at the top of a list of things Shannon wanted to do now or ever. "Sorry, Tara. Maybe another time," she lied.

There was a teasing glint in Ward's eyes, as if he was about to test her earlier pronouncement.

"Maybe Shannon would just like to take a stroll around the place. Get a closer look at some of our prized saddle horses."

Shannon wished she could mount any horse he picked, sit gracefully in the saddle like a true horse-woman and gallop along beside him, but such a fantasy belied the truth. She wasn't even sure which side of a horse was the proper one to mount.

"Would you like to go see Calico?" the little girl asked eagerly, ready to take over the guide duties from her father.

"Maybe a little later," Ward said smoothly.

"Why not right now?" Tara argued. "You said we could show her around after dinner."

"Tara," Beth intervened. "I think you'd better think about helping me in the kitchen while your dad and Shannon have a little time to themselves."

The way Beth said it made Shannon uncomfortable. It was as if his sister were suggesting there was something romantic going on between her and Ward. Shannon suddenly wished she hadn't come at all. What sense did it make to slip into an intimacy with this inviting man that had no future for either of them?

She'd never been one to run away, but she stiffened as Ward put a gentle hand on her arm and guided her out of the house.

"Let's take a walk. I want to show you a private place of mine."

The way his eyes smiled at her created an intimacy between them that frightened her. As they walked through a green cathedral of tall, majestic trees toward the sound of rushing water, she was aware of an instinctive warning not to let her feelings be swept away into deep waters for this man, but in her heart, she suspected that it might already be too late.

Chapter Five

Ward measured the steps of his long legs as they headed down a narrow well-worn path away from the house through a wooded area cupping the green meadow. It had been a long time since he'd been out on a Sunday walk with a woman companion. Several times, his sister had invited single ladies from the church to come for Sunday dinner, but he'd finally put his foot down about her matchmaking. He knew she liked Judy and approved of her brother dating someone from the church. She'd obviously been surprised, and maybe a little disappointed, that he hadn't followed up on the opportunities the pretty brunette had given him to deepen their friendship.

"I'll get myself a girl when you find yourself a fellow," he had facetiously bargained with her. Although he enjoyed feminine company, his life was so full with the ranch, his daughter and the church that he hadn't gone out of his way for that kind of companionship—until now.

When he told Beth he was bringing a woman home after church service, she had raised an eyebrow but held her curiosity in check. He knew his sister was very perceptive about people, and he was glad she had been her usual friendly self during dinner. Ward suspected she'd seen beneath Shannon's polished exterior to the lonely soul that lay beneath, and he was delighted Tara had taken to Shannon with such enthusiasm.

He smiled at Shannon as they walked. "My family likes you."

"I'm glad," she said simply and truthfully. It was nice to have instant acceptance without straining to do and say the right thing. Most of the time she felt she had to play the role of successful modern woman in the company of others, and it was a rare experience to let down those social barriers.

"You haven't said much about yourself," he said as he studied her face. He couldn't help but notice how totally beautiful she was when she was relaxed. He wished her mouth and eyes would always hold the softness he saw in them at that moment, but even as he watched, his words brought a change in her expression. The muscles in her lovely high cheeks tightened. Guarded. Almost defensive. He'd noticed that reaction before when he'd invited information about herself.

"There's not much to say. My parents are dead. I've been successful in my career, and I value my independence above everything else." She didn't add that the one serious relationship she'd had a few years ago had ended badly and that she had determined then not to make that kind of mistake again.

It was obvious she'd been hurt and didn't trust people.

He replied thoughtfully, "Sometimes when we strive too hard to be independent what we are really doing is avoiding an enriching involvement with people, society and life in general."

"Dependence is weakness," she countered strongly. "I hate it."

"Dependency can be a very nice thing," he argued just as firmly. "None of us are totally sufficient unto ourselves. We need each other and God in our lives."

She set her chin firmly. "If you depend upon yourself, you're never disappointed."

He smiled wanly. "I'm afraid I've disappointed myself a good many times trying to satisfy my own ego."

"A healthy ego can be a good thing," she countered.

Not if ego stands for edging God out, he thought, but didn't pursue the subject. She was like a skittish colt when it came to spiritual beliefs, and he sighed, knowing it would take time and patience to lead her to the Lord. And time with her was something he couldn't count on. She could be out of his life as quickly as she'd entered it. If only— Then he stopped himself from trying to force something that wasn't meant to be. *Thy will, not mine, be done.*

They made their way through thick stands of quivering aspen trees and wild shrubs until they reached a slow-moving mountain stream. The water was clear, and shallow enough for them to see the bottom as it rippled over glistening rocks and made lazy eddies along the bank.

Playfully, Ward took Shannon's hand and pulled her

toward the water. "Come on. Let's cross over to the other side."

Her gaze scanned the stream in both directions. "Where's the bridge?"

"Right there." He pointed toward the stream. "We'll hop across on those."

"What?" She stared at glistening wet rocks barely rising above the water. "You have to be kidding."

"Nope." Without waiting for her consent, he knelt in front of her. "You'll have to take those off," he said as he unbuckled her sandals. "The soles on your shoes might cause you to fall."

"Are you sure about this?" She could visualize herself trying to hop across the stream on those rocks and falling facedown in the rushing water. "Is this some kind of initiation?"

"Kinda." He grinned.

"What about your shoes?" she protested as she scrunched her bare toes in the damp ground.

"They've got rubber soles. Come on." He took her hand and led her down the edge of the stream. "Just hop quickly from one rock to the other."

"What if I slip?"

"Oh, you don't want to do that."

"But what if I do?"

"The water will be deliciously cold." He grinned. "Don't worry, I'll keep hold of you." With that, he put his hands on her waist and urged her to step out in front of him on the first stone.

She squealed as the icy water hit her bare feet.

"Go! Go!" he urged.

Lifting her feet high, she stepped quickly from one

stone to the next. She almost made it all the way across without mishap, but the very last stone was slippery with moss, and one foot spun out from under her. She would have fallen fanny first into the water if Ward hadn't quickly lifted her up on the bank.

They both laughed as they threw themselves down on some warm sandstone rocks, and she tucked her feet under her to get warm.

She felt strangely exhilarated, almost a stranger to herself.

Sitting beside her, Ward wondered at himself for daring to bring her here to his special place. But the luminous glow on her face and the sparkle in her eyes reassured him that he'd made the right decision.

He often came to this spot to sit quietly on these rocks and mediate while his soul drew in the beauty of God's creations. As sunlight bathed quivering aspen leaves with gold, he watched spears of light dance through branches of tall ponderosa pines and white-trunked aspen. To him, the muted sound of flowing water was like a heavenly chorus that always filled his ears with song. Fragile wild blue flowers grew along the bank and among the scattered stones. Impulsively, he reached over, picked one and slipped it behind one of Shannon's ears.

"A pretty flower for a pretty lady."

She laughed, and for a moment, as she sat there with the blossom in her hair, he glimpsed the vivacious young girl she must have been before the world had had its way with her. His chest suddenly tightened because he knew there was no way he could hold on to this fleeting moment, but he drew in a thankful breath that he had met her, however briefly, and prayed that someday she might realize she was God's precious child.

With her eyes soft and smiling at him, she touched the blue flower. "What kind is it?"

"It's a forget-me-not."

She didn't know whether he was teasing or telling her the truth, but she wasn't going to go there. It didn't matter.

She drew in a deep breath and leaned back on her arms. "This is nice."

"Was it worth the cold footbath?"

"Absolutely."

Her genuine pleasure shone in the graceful posture of her body and the lift of her head as she let her eyes take in the flight of a blue jay returning to his nest in the needled crown of a blue spruce tree. Maybe she would remember this moment when she got back to the demanding city, he thought, and it would strengthen her to face whatever challenges lay ahead. Even though she was in denial that she needed anyone's help—even the Lord's—he intended to keep praying for her, anyway.

Feeling closer to him than she had to anyone for as long as she could remember, Shannon asked about his childhood and was pleased when he willingly talked about his time away from the ranch.

"I couldn't wait to get away from home. I didn't want to have anything to do with my father's plan to turn the ranch to the breeding and raising of Appaloosa horses. I left him and Beth to manage everything while

I attended a small agricultural college in northern Colorado.''

He didn't tell her that he'd drifted away from the teachings of his Christian family, that his life at college was a living example of the prodigal son's parable. While in college he married without any spiritual foundation for the union.

"My parents died while I was in college, and when my wife, Valerie, suddenly passed away from cancer, I brought our daughter back to the ranch to raise.'' He took a deep breath. "I got my life back on track, thank the Lord. Tara loves it here, and Beth is wonderful with her.''

"She's a lovely little girl and seems to take to people easily.''

"Not all people.'' Ward said with a grin. "Just those from Hollywood, Disneyland and Sea World. She's really got a thing about California.''

"Then you'll have to bring her out for a visit.''

"Yes, maybe I will,'' he agreed, even though he knew that would never happen. It wasn't likely Shannon Hensley would have time for entertaining a chance acquaintance of a few days when she resumed her normal busy life. "Well, we'd better head back.''

She nodded. "I'm sorry you have to make another trip to the school and back.''

"No problem. I need to take in some produce that Beth has collected from the other ranchers. The Red Cross needs all the donations they can get.''

He held out a hand and helped her to her feet. "Are you ready for another footbath?''

She grimaced, looking down. "I think they're still blue."

"Then we'd better do it this way." Before she could react, he'd swung her up in his arms. "I'll carry you across?"

"Can you…can you keep your footing?" she stammered.

"I guess we'll find out," he said as he carefully navigated his way into the water and stepped onto the first stone.

The thought of being dumped into the ice-cold rushing stream was enough to make Shannon close her eyes and rest her head against his chest as he gingerly stepped from one rock to the next. Once he wavered slightly, and she tightened her grip on his neck. The steady rising and falling of his breath was reassuring, and she let herself relax against him.

When he set her down safely on the other side, he laughingly tipped her chin up. "See, sometimes trust and dependence are good things."

As his eyes locked with hers, she was startled by an unfamiliar willingness to agree. "That depends on who's doing the depending on whom."

Impulsively, she raised up on bare feet and kissed his cheek.

He laughed. "Well, that's one way to have the last word."

He kept his arm lightly around her waist as they walked to the house.

Shannon was surprised when both Beth and Ward invited her to take advantage of their spare room and remain at the ranch instead of returning to the evacuation center.

"Thank you, but I really have to be on the spot when the Chimney Ridge road opens to make sure that Pete's Towing Service goes after my car. I want to be ready to leave as soon as they allow traffic on the main highway."

"That may not be for a few more days," Beth warned her. Shannon noticed Ward had remained silent, and her chest tightened as she realized she might never see him or his family again. At the thought, something close to panic swept through her as she realized she might be falling for this churchgoing, straitlaced rancher. No, that wasn't going to happen. She was no dewy-eyed female who was going to let her emotions become tangled in an impossible relationship. She had enjoyed a pleasant afternoon, and that was that.

As Ward drove her to Beaver Junction, he didn't comment on her refusal to stay at the ranch. It was probably for the best all the way around. Logic told him it was better to keep some distance between them. Putting their basic differences and beliefs aside for a few hours was one thing, but pursuing any kind of a continuing relationship was out of the question. Their approaches to life were at opposite ends of the spectrum.

The easy companionship that had been with them during the afternoon dissipated as soon as they entered the overcrowded school. Once again, Shannon was caught up in the tension of worried adults, fretful children and overworked volunteers. Everyone was showing the strain of the endless waiting and uncertain outcome of a dragon fire that refused to die.

The update was not good. Higher temperatures and low humidity caused the burning acres to expand. A call had gone out for more firefighters. The number of air tankers dropping flame-retardant "slurry" and runs made by helicopters releasing big buckets of water had been increased. Some paratroopers had been dropped in remote areas to begin a backburn so the encroaching fire would run out of fuel when it met the blackened area.

Shannon didn't understand any of the tactics of forest firefighting and was filled with an anger that had its basis in fear. "Can't they do something more? How long is this going to go on?"

Ward's calm assurance when he told her to keep the faith landed on deaf ears and made her realize how worlds apart they were. She wanted to do something, take some action, not depend upon some fickle fate to solve her problems.

Ward saw the fear in her eyes and the stubborn set of her mouth. The tender, laughing young woman who sat beside the creek with him was gone. He wanted to take her in his arms and soothe away her fears, but he knew that she would reject any such action.

As she watched him walk away and disappear into the cafeteria with the donated produce, she almost ran after him. The impulse to ask him to take her to the ranch threatened her common sense, and she stiffened against the temptation. No use going down that road, she told herself.

"Miss Hensley."

She turned and saw Kenny's father with some papers in his hand. Grinning broadly, he held one out to her.

"What is it?" she asked, puzzled. Usually daily printed bulletins were left on a table for people to pick up.

"It's a little newspaper. They let me use the school computer, scanner and printer. I wrote up some stories and news items about some of the people here—and look! Here's the drawing you made. I gave you credit and everything."

It took her by surprise. At first, she stared at the sketch she'd made of the old man in the rocking chair, not knowing whether to be angry, flattered or indifferent.

"You're not mad or anything, are you?"

She was surprised when she found a feeble smile tugging at her lips. "No. It's just unexpected."

"I'm going to put out a second one tomorrow. May I use another one of your sketches? It really adds a lot."

In any other circumstances, she would have instantly refused, but she said uncertainly, "I guess so."

This kind of public exposure to her doodling was both satisfying and a little embarrassing, but if it would help anyone endure this trying situation, she didn't see how she could refuse. She offered him the sketches she'd made of the sewing ladies and the mother with her child.

"These are great," he said with enthusiasm. "Maybe I could do a story on you to go along with the drawings."

"No." She shook her head. "And you don't have

to mention my name at all. There's nothing about me that would be of interest to anyone."

"I wouldn't be so sure about that. Everyone knows that it was Pokey who made you lose control of your car. We're all glad that a certain eligible rancher has taken you under his wing."

Shannon instantly stiffened. The word *eligible* put a slant on his remark that made her uncomfortable. Did everyone think she was interested in Ward Dawson in that way? She certainly wasn't—was she?

Ward was asking himself the same kind of question when Laura Cozzins thanked him for the large box of donated goods and said, "Bless you. Tell Beth we'll make good use of everything." Then she gave him a knowing smile. "I know you took Shannon to the ranch to spend the day. Did you have a good time?"

"Yes and no," he said honestly, not knowing exactly how he felt about the afternoon. Sunday dinner was pleasant enough, and he was pleased with the way both Tara and Beth had related to Shannon. What troubled him was how suddenly the intimacy he'd experienced sitting with Shannon had dissipated. She seemed almost impatient to return to the school, as if she couldn't wait to put some distance between them.

"I guess Miss Shannon Hensley found ranch life a little boring," he told Laura with a wry smile. "Or maybe just a few hours with me was enough. She turned down Beth's offer of our spare bedroom, as if being around me and my family was less inviting than returning to the crowded gym."

"Sounds as if your pride is smarting just a wee bit."

"I suppose it could be that," he admitted. He wasn't

about to tell her how close he'd come to taking the city gal in his arms and kissing her. Even now, the memory of her soft smile and the flower in her hair sent a warmth through him.

"I guess I picked up some wrong signals."

"Could be you just need to give her a little more time to get to know you better."

"I don't think that sticking around Beaver Junction is in her itinerary," Ward said honestly. "I'd have to hog-tie her to keep her one minute longer once the roads are open."

"Maybe not," Laura said with genuine optimism. "But in any case, we'll pray for God's blessing upon her, and know that His plan is the best one, after all." She eyed him frankly. "You do believe that He has a plan for each of us, don't you?"

"Yes, I do," he answered readily. "But sometimes I wonder why the dear Lord has to take us around the bend in the road before He shows us where we're going."

She laughed and patted his shoulder. "Just fasten your seat belt and let Him do the driving."

Ward didn't see Shannon as he made his way out of the school, and he decided it was probably best to leave things the way they were. By the time he got back to the ranch, Ted was in the kitchen having a late dinner. The young man looked tired and worried and shook his head when Ward asked how things were at his grandmother's place.

"Not good. Smoke and ashes are heavy in the air even though the fire is not directly threatening her place—yet. Grams has trouble breathing. I tried to get her to evacuate, but she's a stubborn old gal. Ever since my grandpa died, she'd held the place together with pure grit and nothing else.''

''Is there anything I can do?''

''Not at the moment. We'll just have to wait and see.'' Ted eyed Ward as he sat down at the table. ''Beth said you had that pretty California gal out for dinner.''

Ward nodded.

''And?'' Ted prodded.

''And what?''

''Come on, guy. Give. Did you two hit it off, or what?''

Ward pretended innocence as he answered, ''I don't know what you mean.''

''Did you like her? Does she like you?'' Ted demanded impatiently.

''The answer to both your questions is I don't know. Besides, it doesn't matter. She'll be first in line when they open the Elkhorn road to traffic.''

''Not in that fancy sports car, she won't,'' Ted said flatly. Then seeing Ward's expression, he asked, ''Didn't you know? I was talking to a fellow in Beaver Junction a little while ago. He said her car slipped off that rock ledge this afternoon. Nothing left but a pile of twisted metal at the bottom of the canyon.''

Ward's heart tightened as a deep compassion for the vulnerable young woman with the soft blue-gray eyes flooded through him. He could see her ashen face when she heard the news. He wished he could have been the one to tell her. She needed someone to hold her close and tell her it was going to be all right.

Chapter Six

Shannon was in the cafeteria, helping to clear off some of the tables after the breakfast rush, when Ward came in the next morning. As he walked toward her, she thought he was looking at her strangely, as if searching her face for some hint as to what she was thinking. Something about his purposeful manner made her stiffen. The curve of his lips was at odds with the serious, questioning glint in his eyes.

"Good morning." He greeted her in a pleasant enough tone, but she caught the hint of a question in it. She wasn't fooled. He had something on his mind.

"You're here bright and early."

"I finished my chores early and thought we might take a little walk before the day's rush begins."

"A walk?"

"And a little talk," he admitted, a shadow flickering in his dark-brown eyes. He knew from her manner that she hadn't heard the bad news.

Her mouth was suddenly dry. "All right."

As they walked across the school grounds, Ward tried to keep the conversation light. The morning sun was a bright apricot, promising another hot day with no rain in sight. They could hear the protesting barks of pet dogs confined to kennels, and the playground was already filled with children expending their energies on swings and slides.

He pointed out a small football stadium. "The fighting Beavers have played many a tough game on that field."

Shannon only half-listened to his story about the time the Beavers almost won a trophy but lost the game in the last two seconds of play. She was perceptive enough to know that he was stalling. Finally, she faced him squarely and demanded, "What is it, Ward?"

"I have some bad news." He knew there was no way to soften the truth so he took her hand and said, "I'm truly sorry, Shannon. Your car broke free of the rock ledge sometime yesterday afternoon. It crashed and burned at the bottom of the ravine."

"It's...it's gone? Everything's gone?"

"I'm afraid so."

Even though she had tried to prepare herself for such a happening, every fiber of her being fought against an overpowering feeling of helplessness. Now if the roads opened in the next hour, she wouldn't have any transportation out of Beaver Junction or to any other place she might decide to go.

"The great blessing is that you weren't in it," he reminded her. "You could have been, you know."

She nodded and took a deep breath. Maintaining

self-control was an ingrained habit from the time she was a little girl. When faced with the frightening news that they were moving again, leaving behind the few friends and a familiar place, she had learned to hide her hurts and fears. She was used to hiding behind the pretense that she could handle anything that came along. "Well, I guess that's that. I'd better find a telephone and see what I can do to solve the problem."

"What can I do to help?"

"Nothing, I'm afraid," she said as she withdrew her hand from his. Keeping her feelings hidden was important in the business world, and though she was in no position to finance another car, she wasn't about to let him know it. "I'd better walk down to the pay phone and make some calls. I'll have to call the insurance company and the bank. I suppose I can find a used car for sale that will get me back to Los Angeles."

"Maybe not in Beaver Junction, but Elkhorn has all kinds of car sale lots."

Ward had expected to see some tears and a need for reassurance when she heard the bad news, but obviously she didn't need his strong shoulder to cry on. He felt a little foolish when he realized that replacing the expensive sports car wasn't going to be a problem for her, and she could hitch a ride into Elkhorn when the road opened and buy another one. He felt foolish for having entertained the idea that she might need him in this situation. He should have remembered that one of the first things she ever said to him was, "I can handle things nicely by myself."

She was silent on the walk down the hill to Main Street, and he decided he'd stick around and make sure she got things settled to her satisfaction. "I'll have a cup of coffee at the diner while you make your calls."

"All right. I shouldn't be long," she said with a confidence that belied the trembling of her hand as she took a small address book out of her purse.

He nodded and disappeared inside the diner.

As she called her bank, she wished she hadn't lived so close to the limits of her paycheck every month. Rent for her leased apartment was only enough to cover her mortgage payment. She had arranged for the rent to be deposited in her account and a draft drawn for the mortgage company. No telling how long it would be before the insurance company settled a claim on her accident. It certainly wouldn't be in the next day or two. They'd have to investigate the accident and make out reports. She was worried that the bank might not be inclined to make a loan to an unemployed woman. Still, she had no choice.

Her call went quickly through on her telephone charge card, and in a few short minutes she was given information on her account. In horror, she learned that the rent on her apartment had not been banked, and since she had arranged for the mortgage company to draw the amount due directly from her account, she was dangerously close to being overdrawn. She barely had money enough in her savings to cover her bills.

She hung up the phone, leaned against the booth and fought a rising nausea. Talking to a loan officer about financing another car in her present financial straits was out of the question. *Broke. Jobless. Trapped.*

She covered her face with her hands, and tears that she had been holding back suddenly began to flow.

Like the sudden bursting of a dam, torrents of tears poured down her face, and her shoulders heaved with sobs. The last few days had depleted her physical and emotional reserves.

Ward had been sitting by a front window where he'd been watching her make the call. Judy had brought him a cup of coffee and done her best to engage him in some conversation about the fire, but he only made the expected superficial answers.

Judy followed his gaze out the window, and when she saw Shannon in the phone booth, she said rather peevishly, "I guess you've got something else on your mind. Everyone at the church is talking about it, you know."

"Really? I thought the Bible had something to say about gossiping being the tool of the devil? And I think it also says that we are to help those in need."

"Well, it seems to be a little more than just Christian charity the way you've been looking after Shannon Hensley," Judy snapped and flounced to the kitchen.

Ward glanced out the window again, and saw Shannon still standing in the glass booth, but her shoulders were shaking as she covered her face with her hand. He jerked to his feet, ran out the door and covered the ground with long strides.

He knocked on the glass. "Shannon? What's wrong?"

She lifted her tear-streaked face, opened the booth's door and went into his arms without hesitation. He was taken aback by the way she clung to him. He didn't know what had happened to shatter her protective veneer, but she was like a frightened child, desperately needing love and reassurance.

Her fears poured out like a gusher as she related the details of her phone conversation.

His hands soothed her trembling shoulders, and he bent his head close to hers. "Hey, it's going to be all right. It's going to be all right."

"I don't know what to do." Shannon couldn't believe all this was happening to her. Even when she'd lost her important executive position, she'd refused to accept defeat. All that prideful confidence in herself had been slowly eroding, and her life suddenly seemed out of control. "I just don't know what to do," she repeated in a trembling voice.

"You need time to think things out. You're going home with me." The minute the words were out, Ward knew they were the right ones. In his morning prayers, he always asked for divine guidance for the day, and at that moment, he believed that the Lord was leading him in the way that he should go. He wiped the tears from her wet cheeks. "The ranch is a great place to touch base with yourself." *And God,* he silently added.

Tara was ecstatic when Ward returned to the ranch with Shannon later in the day. The little girl clapped her hands and gave Shannon a big hug. "I prayed to God that you'd come back," she said. "And here you are!"

Ward suppressed a chuckle. Leave it to his daughter to parade her faith in front of anyone.

"We're happy to have you." Beth smiled at Ward in a knowing way, as if she wasn't surprised to learn that Shannon Hensley wasn't going to disappear from their lives as suddenly as she had appeared. "You're welcome to stay as long as you like."

"I shouldn't have to impose on you for very long," Shannon said quickly, having recovered her usual stubborn willfulness to shape her life the way she wanted it, regardless of the circumstances. "Just a few days."

"Let me show you our spare room. Don't feel that you have to carry out any guest obligations. Join the family when you want to, or just be by yourself. Feel free to enjoy the peace and quiet any way you like. I imagine you could use some of that about now."

Shannon sent Ward a grateful look. Embarrassed by the way she had fallen apart, she didn't know what to say to this sudden outreaching of his family. She'd never been dependent on someone else's generosity before, and their open loving kindness was foreign to her.

"While you settle in, Shannon, I'll head out to the stables. We're still maintaining a vigil on Calico," Ward said.

"Why is she taking so long?" Tara asked in a complaining voice. "I'm getting tired of waiting."

Ward playfully pulled on one of her pigtails. "Not as tired as Calico, I'll bet. You'll have to learn that you can't hurry Mother Nature. When the baby colt is ready, he'll make his appearance."

"It's not going to be a he," Tara announced with all the conviction of a stubborn child. "It's going to be a she. And her name is going to be Princess."

Ward laughed. "Well, I'd better go check and see if Princess is about to make an appearance. I'll leave you in good hands, Shannon. See you at lunch."

For an absurd moment, she almost asked to go with him. Somehow he had become an anchor in a world that had turned upside down, and there was something about him that reached out to her on levels she didn't understand. Her lost feeling must have shown on her face, because Beth quickly moved to her side.

"It'll be nice to have another woman in the house," she said, smiling. "Come on, I'll show you the upstairs." She eyed Shannon's small overnight bag. "Here, let me carry that for you. Is this everything you brought?"

Shannon swallowed hard and nodded. Replacing everything she'd lost was going to be another draining expense she could ill afford. "Everything else was in the car."

"That's too bad, but things can always be replaced. Ward said when he first saw the car, he wasn't sure he could get you out in time. It was amazing the way it got hung up on those rocks, wasn't it?"

"Yes, I guess I was pretty lucky."

"Maybe it was more than luck," Beth countered.

As they climbed the stairs, Tara grabbed Shannon's hand. "You can borrow any of my stuff," she offered with childish generosity.

"Thank you, Tara. That's very nice of you."

"I'm glad you're going to be next to my room. We can talk at night." Tara said it with such satisfaction that Shannon suspected the little girl probably put up a nightly fuss about going to bed and turning out the light.

"The guest bedroom is at the back of the house," Beth said when they reached the upper hall. "It has a nice large window overlooking the meadow. I know you'll enjoy the view. Watching the young colts scampering beside their mothers is always a joy and a lift to the spirits.'' She eyed Shannon. ''It's different than the city, but in some ways just as exciting.''

''I can teach you how to ride a horse,'' Tara said.

''I don't think there'll be that much time—''

''My dad taught me in only a couple of days,'' Tara insisted. ''Besides, I don't see why you can't stay a long, long time.''

''Tara, that's enough,'' Beth said firmly. ''Don't pester. We're just happy Shannon came back to pay us a visit, aren't we?''

Tara nodded, but there was a determined frown on her little forehead that hinted she had more to say on the subject. She pointed out her bedroom as they passed down the hall. It was furnished with pretty maple furniture and decorated with childish clutter. ''If you get scared in the night, you can come crawl in bed with me.''

''Now, Tara, don't be thinking you can do likewise,'' Beth warned her, giving Shannon a knowing smile.

She led the way into a small bedroom that was furnished with a single bed and a matching oak chest and dresser. A blue, yellow and pink floral bedspread harmonized with simple cotton curtains hanging at the window. One chair with soft cushions was placed beside a small table that held a reading lamp and a Bible.

''The bathroom is at the end of the hall. I'll put out an extra towel for you.''

At any other time in her life, Shannon would have

been critical of the hard bed, small quarters and the inconvenience of not having a private bathroom, but compared to the evacuation center, these accommodations were a luxury.

"Do you want to see all the stuff in my room now?" Tara asked eagerly. "And then I'll take you out to the barn and—"

Beth quickly interrupted her with a reminder that morning chores were still waiting, and she suggested that it might be better to save the tour until after lunch.

"You run along, Tara, and collect the eggs in the chicken coop. Maybe we'll bake some cookies later."

"My favorite kind?" Tara coaxed. "I bet Shannon likes peanut butter the best, too."

"Absolutely," Shannon responded, and Tara's eyes glowed.

Beth laughed and scooted Tara out the door. Then she turned to Shannon. "Feel free to rest, join us in the kitchen or just wander around. Ward and Ted will show up at noon and be as hungry as bears. I'd better see to getting some grub ready to put on the table."

Shannon knew she should offer to help, but she couldn't make herself do it. "I think I'll rest."

"Good idea." Beth paused, as if searching for the right thing to say. "It's been a long time since I've seen my brother with a swing in his step." She eyed Shannon. "I hope I'm not talking out of turn, but I can't help but feel protective."

Protective? Did Beth think Shannon had designs on her brother? Was she warning her to keep hands off? Shannon silently bristled. Getting seriously involved with any man was certainly not on her list of things to do at the moment. True enough, she appreciated Ward's friendliness in this dark moment of her life, and she couldn't deny that she found him attractive, but she wasn't planning on making anything permanent out of his attention to her.

"What do you mean, protective?" Shannon asked pointedly.

"Well, I guess I'm concerned that he may get hurt again. He married impulsively while still in college, and the match wasn't a good one for him or Tara's mother. When he came back to the ranch after her death, he had to find himself again, and with the Lord's help, he has." She smiled at Shannon. "Nothing would please me more if he found the right soul mate for his life, but the Bible warns us not to 'yoke unevenly.' Do you understand what I'm saying?"

"Clearly. And you have nothing to worry about, I assure you. I have no intention of 'yoking,' as you put it, with your brother or anyone else. I like Ward and appreciate his kindness to me, but I'll be gone in a few days and put all this behind me."

Beth nodded. "I'm sorry if I spoke out of turn. This is such a stressful time for everyone that it's easy to say the wrong thing. All of us are glad to have you here. Please rest, and come downstairs whenever you want company." She smiled as she left the room and closed the door.

Shannon remained standing in the middle of the floor for a long minute, like a rudderless boat. As she slowly turned, she glimpsed her reflection in the dresser mirror and froze. She stared at the pale face, heavy-lidded eyes and listless hair, searching for some recognition.

The woman was a stranger. Where was the successful, well-groomed Shannon Hensley? As she stared at her reflection, a flash of defiance rose within her.

No! She clenched her fists. This defeated, frightened image wasn't her. She'd weathered setbacks and disappointments before. Taking care of herself had been a part of her mind-set from the time she was in grade school and her parents left her for nearly a year at a strict boarding academy. She had looked after herself then, and she would look after herself now. She appreciated the generous help she was getting from Ward and his family, but she wasn't about to accept it any longer than necessary. Maybe her next call to the employment agency would be a positive one, and come hell or high water, she'd get back to California for that interview.

She walked to the window that looked out on the stables and corrals and saw Ward swing up into the saddle of a beautiful dark-brown and white Appaloosa. Something inside her warmed to the beauty of horse and man moving in graceful rhythm across the rich green meadow. Despite her resolve, it was a scene she would hold in her memory always. As she turned away from the window she knew this place, this home and this family would always create a sense of longing for something she had never experienced in her life, and if the pattern held true, she never would.

Chapter Seven

The sun was setting when Shannon awoke from a deep afternoon nap. Her first awareness was the tangy smell of something being barbecued floating up from the yard. As she sat on the edge of the bed, she was disoriented for a moment. Then she remembered where she was. Out of the goodness of his Christian heart, Ward had brought her to his home. She felt somewhat like a fraud, imposing upon him and his sister this way. Because it had always been important for her to pay her own way, she was uncomfortable when others did things for her, secretly feeling that she didn't deserve it.

Hearing muffled voices and laughter, she walked to the window, but she couldn't see anyone. She had missed lunch, and the sun was already disappearing behind high barren peaks. For a moment, she almost gave in to the impulse to crawl back in bed and ignore the tempting odor of cooking and the inviting laughter.

Then she heard Ward's deep laugh, and something inside her instantly responded. She wanted to go downstairs and be with him.

A glance in the mirror told her she wasn't fit company for anyone. After peering down the hall, she stepped out of her room and stealthily made her way to the bathroom. She couldn't believe how large it was, spacious enough to offer a separate shower and large, old-fashioned tub.

She opted for a bath and filled the tub almost to the top. Then she eased down into it and sank up to her neck in warm soapy water scented by a rose bubble bath she found in a large bottle placed by the tub. As she leaned back and closed her eyes, she let her whole body and mind rest in the pleasure of the moment. She had never felt such luxury or entertained this kind of deep appreciation for the simple act of taking a bath. With a new awareness she realized that the simple pleasures of life became invaluable when she was denied them.

As she dressed and plaited her hair in a French braid, she was glad she had packed a second pair of designer jeans and a summer pullover top in her overnight bag. Just thinking about the new clothes, still unpaid for, that were now charred cinders in a wrecked car destroyed her momentary sense of well-being. Even though she told herself everything could be replaced in time, the question of when and how long it might take was enough to dampen her spirits.

Quietly she went downstairs and followed the sound of voices to a wide brick patio stretched across the back of the house. Ward was sitting with Ted at a picnic table, and he rose to his feet the minute he saw her, giving her a broad welcoming smile.

"I was hoping you'd feel like joining us."

"I didn't intend to sleep the day away," she apologized. She didn't want him to think she was avoiding contact with him or his family.

"No problem. I've put some chicken on the grill, and Beth has baked potatoes and the makings of a fresh salad from her garden. How does that sound? She and Tara are busy preparing strawberries for dessert."

"Maybe I should go in the kitchen and help?" Shannon offered uncertainly.

"Oh, no." Ward laughed and shook his head. "You don't want to invade Beth's domain without invitation. She's been known to hang up intruders by their thumbs." He winked at her. "Better you sit down and have a glass of lemonade."

Ted had also risen to his feet, looking a little uncomfortable in Shannon's presence. He shot a quick look at Ward, then looked at her as if he wasn't sure what to say or do. Shannon had the feeling they might have been talking about her before she interrupted them.

Ted mumbled self-consciously, "Nice to see you again."

"Pour her a glass of lemonade, Ted, while I check the chicken."

She said thank-you when the young man handed her a glass, then she casually followed Ward to a large brick grill at one end of the patio. Sounds of juice popping in the fire mingled with the sizzle of chicken as he brushed the pieces with a rich barbecue sauce.

"I hope you're hungry," he said. "And rested."

She nodded, but Ward didn't believe her. The nap had done her good, but there were still faint shadows under her eyes and a tightness around her mouth. He had a strong urge to draw her close and assure her once again that everything was going to be all right.

A little earlier, Beth had suggested that having Shannon around for even a short time might not have been such a good idea, after all. "There's some kind of an undercurrent going on between you two."

He had made light of her remark, but he knew Shannon Hensley had challenged him from the first moment he laid eyes on her. There was something about her spunky bravado that appealed to him, and almost immediately he had recognized her tough exterior for the sham it was. Underneath that sophisticated, independent veneer, he glimpsed a child of God who had fought too many lonely battles. He was taken by her soft eyes, her vulnerable smile and the way she held her head up when she was afraid. Yes, there was no doubt about it. He was attracted to her in a way he hadn't been with other female acquaintances. Maybe this was some kind of test to see how dedicated he was to his determination not to marry anyone who didn't believe in the presence of God being as close as one's breath.

At that moment Tara bounded out the door. "You're here, Shannon," she cried. "Aunt Beth said you were probably still sleeping. You should see the strawberry shortcake we made. You can have as big a piece as you like. Even two! And—"

"Whoa, girl." Ward laughingly cut her off. "I bet you're the one hankering for two pieces."

"Well, maybe," she agreed with a sheepish smile. "I even snuck a taste or two while we were putting on the whipped cream. Just to make sure it was okay for company. Only Shannon isn't company, is she? 'Cause she's staying here, just like family."

Shannon's chest suddenly felt tight. The little girl's innocent exuberance made her feel more out of place than ever. Had she made some kind of terrible commitment coming here? She could tell from the deepening furrow in Ward's forehead that his daughter's remarks were disturbing him, too. She didn't know how to respond without seeming totally ungrateful for their hospitality.

Fortunately, Beth called both Tara and Ted to come and help bring out some dishes, so Shannon and Ward had a moment alone.

"You'll have to forgive Tara," Ward said quietly. "Never thinks before she speaks. You should be glad she likes you. My daughter always lets everyone know exactly how she feels, and sometimes it can be darn right embarrassing. We've all turned beet red when she shows her lack of judgment about saying certain things even if they're true."

"You mean she hasn't learned the art of lying?"

"There's a difference between lying and refraining from saying things that hurt someone else."

Shannon thought for a moment. "I think I'd rather know the truth and be hurt."

"Sometimes it's difficult to know the truth," Ward replied honestly. If she was asking how he felt about her, he didn't have the answer. "I guess that's where trust and faith come in."

"I guess I've always had a short supply of both of those."

"That's all right." He touched her arm gently. "Maybe I've got enough for both of us," he surprised himself by saying, and was glad his sister wasn't around to hear the remark. At least, he hoped she hadn't heard, but when Beth came out of the house at that moment, she gave him a searching look.

"The chicken's ready," he told her, as if he thought that would answer the question in her eyes.

When the picnic table was loaded with food, they sat down and held hands while Ward said the blessing. As Shannon listened to him pray, she was struck by the familiar tone he used in talking about the Almighty. If she hadn't known better, she would have thought he was speaking to some close friend sitting at the table with them.

The meal was a pleasant one full of humor, with Ward and Ted exchanging friendly gibes and telling stories on each other. She learned something about the routine at the ranch and was surprised that Ward had more hired hands than Ted. At the moment, they were all helping with the fire, so the burden of the daily chores fell on Ward and Ted's shoulders. From the talk, Shannon could tell that Beth handled all the business end of the family's thriving sale of Appaloosas throughout the whole Rocky Mountain region.

Beth refused Shannon's offer to help with the cleanup but accepted Ted's offer to carry in the dishes from the table.

"Well, then, Shannon, would you like to go with me

and Tara to check on Calico?'' Ward asked, delighted with the way Shannon was relaxed and smiling.

When she said yes, Tara grabbed Shannon's hand and skipped along at her side as they walked to the stables. The little girl chatted all the way, and Ward sent Shannon an amused smile that showed the deep affection he had for his outgoing, confident little daughter.

''Did you know a daddy horse is called a stallion? And a mama horse is called a mare. A little girl horse is a filly, and a little boy horse is a colt.'' She grinned at Shannon, obviously proud as punch to be showing off her knowledge of horses and riding. ''Calico is going to have a filly.''

''We don't know that,'' her father cautioned.

''I know it,'' she answered with the innocent wiseness of a child.

''We'll see,'' Ward said softly.

''Okay,'' Tara answered agreeably, ''but I already told Calico I'm naming her little filly horse Princess. I think she likes it.'' The little girl bubbled happily.

''Well, who am I to argue with feminine logic?''

''What's logic?'' Tara asked, looking at her father and Shannon with a puzzled expression on her freckled face.

Smiling, Shannon answered, ''It's a way of looking at things that most men don't understand.''

Ward held up his hands in mock surrender. ''No fair ganging up on me, ladies. I know when I'm licked.''

Laughing, he led the way into the stable where several horses were stalled. Most of them were standing quietly with their heads hanging over the half gate, but the sorrel mare in the largest end stall was moving about restlessly.

"What's the matter, old girl?" Ward asked as he went into the stall and let his hand move over the pregnant mare's back. He hadn't said anything to Tara, but Calico was almost six weeks over the usual eleven-month gestation period, and he'd been praying that she would deliver without any complications. The mare had been eating very little bran mash, and he was worried that she might be losing weight. If they lost this foal, he knew his daughter would be devastated. Maybe he shouldn't have promised it to her, but the experience of raising her own horse was something he didn't want her to miss.

Tara hung on the gate, chatting away, telling Calico to hurry up and drop the baby. Shannon could tell from Ward's expression that he was concerned about the mare's condition, but he answered his daughter's questions in an upbeat fashion.

"She's getting ready to be a mother," he assured Tara, noticing some physical signs that she was getting ready for nursing. "I'll keep an eye on her, but most mares will foal in the dead of the night without help from anyone," he told Shannon as he came out of the stall and locked the gate.

As they left the stable, he glanced at his watch. "Time for you to start getting ready for bed, Tara." He ignored her groans. "Head back to the house, now, and tell Beth that I'm going to show Shannon around the rest of the place before we turn in."

Tara made a feeble protest, but apparently she knew when her father meant what he said. The little girl surprised Shannon by giving her a big hug. "I really like you...bunches."

"And I like you bunches." Shannon leaned down and impulsively kissed her cheek.

As Tara headed toward the house in a childish skip, Shannon wondered if she had ever been that free and spontaneous as a child.

"You've really made a hit with my daughter," Ward said as he took her arm. "It's amazing how perceptive children are, isn't it?"

"What do you mean?"

"She saw through to the real you right away."

"Oh, and what is the real me?" Shannon asked, a little testily.

"I'm not sure. But Tara seems to be. Anyway, I want to walk you out to the pasture. It's beautiful in the twilight when the moon is just rising. Besides, the exercise will help you relax and sleep better." He didn't add that this nightly ritual lent a spiritual benediction to the end of a busy and sometimes disappointing day.

They walked slowly down a footpath that edged one of the lodgepole fences. Several horses raised their heads as they passed, and Shannon thought they looked almost ethereal in the silver touch of moonlight.

Ward opened a gate and closed it after they had walked through it. Leaving the house, stable and horses behind, they walked into rippling tall grass that held a hushed silence. The shadowy meadow stretched away to darkened peaks that rose in jagged silhouettes against the vaulting night sky.

Shannon said abruptly, "Let's go back."

Ward was startled by the urgency in her voice. Her face looked white and drawn in the moonlight. "What's the matter?"

She bit her lip, not knowing how to explain without sounding like a frightened child. Standing in the middle of an enormous mountain meadow with an endless canopy of a dark sky above was not a pleasant sensation for her. She felt small, insignificant and of little value in this vastness of earth and sky. The endless galaxies that stretched far beyond man's ability to comprehend made a mockery of the importance of one single human life. She tried to express this feeling to Ward.

"It's only a mockery if you don't believe that every breath you draw is important in the divine scheme of things," Ward responded. "One single soul is as important as any of the other wondrous things God has created. When you know that in your heart, Shannon, you'll never feel small and insignificant again."

She shook her head. "I can't believe that anything I do matters to anyone but myself. It would take a miracle for me to feel differently."

"Well, if the good Lord put the stars in heaven and set our little earth spinning in space, I guess He can handle something as challenging as keeping track of Shannon Hensley's precious soul."

"You really believe that, don't you?"

"Yes." He touched her cheek with a fingertip and eased back a strand of hair falling on her forehead. There was so much he wanted to say to her about God's love and the divine plan He had for everyone, but some inner voice cautioned him to move slowly.

Shannon braced herself for a lecture on religious

doctrine, but Ward simply smiled at her. "Come on, I want to show you where I sit and commune with God and nature by myself."

Putting a firm arm around her waist, he guided her to a slight rise in the meadow where several trees had been felled. Their trunks were stripped of bark, and three of them had been laid together like a rustic floor.

"It's my outdoor house, without confining walls, windows and a roof to spoil the magnificent view." He sat down, motioned for her to join him and was surprised when she refused.

"This is your private place, and I think you ought to keep it that way." She couldn't share his beliefs, and by inviting her here, he wanted her to be something she wasn't.

He could tell from the set of her chin it was useless to argue, and any hope of making her feel more comfortable in the awesome expanse of sky and earth faded. "All right, I'll walk you back to the house, and then I'll go check on Calico."

They walked in silence as they made their way through the meadow toward the house. Ward was aware of the sharp tingle of smoke in the air and wondered if that meant the fire was moving closer. The canyons behind the ranch, like the one where Ted's mother lived, would be the first to be invaded if the fire wasn't stopped.

As they passed the stables, they heard a faint whinny. Ward stiffened, stopped and listened.

"Wait here," he told Shannon, as he turned and disappeared into the stable.

Shannon's first impulse was to ignore his order and

follow him, but if it was Calico delivering her foal, she wasn't sure she was up to viewing the process. Watching television medical dramas was as close as she'd ever come to viewing a birthing.

She sat on a bale of hay outside the barn, waiting for him. As the minutes passed and Ward didn't come out, her chest began to tighten. Was something wrong? She knew how much Tara wanted this colt. The little girl would be devastated if something went wrong.

More and more time went by. He'd been gone a long time. Shannon debated whether she should keep on waiting, go inside the stable or return to the house and tell someone what the situation was.

But what was the situation?

Maybe Ward wasn't tending to Calico at all. Something else could be demanding his attention. She'd feel like a fool if she got everyone excited about the mare when Ward's hasty disappearance might be due to a different problem altogether.

Finally, impatient with herself for being so indecisive, she rose to her feet, firmed her steps and made her way into the dimly lighted stable. The noise of restless horses in the stalls echoed loudly in her ears as she cautiously walked past them. She stopped before she reached the brightest light at the end stall, Calico's.

There was no doubt about it. It was Calico's whinny that had brought Ward racing into the stable. Shannon debated whether she should retrace her steps or see for herself what was happening.

"Ward?" she finally called cautiously.

There was a long silence before he answered, "Yes. It's all right, Shannon. Come here."

Slowly she approached the well-lighted stall but didn't see him or the horse until she was close enough to look over the half gate.

Both man and mare were on the straw-covered floor. There was something else, too.

A tiny, bright-eyed newborn raised its head as if impatient to get a first look at the world. Filled with an undescribable swell of emotion, Shannon stared speechless at the beautiful brown-spotted baby horse.

Ward grinned at Shannon from ear to ear. "Say hello to Princess."

"Is she okay?"

"Perfect." He gently stroked the newborn foal with a warm cloth. "Princess is perfect in every way." His eyes suddenly brimmed. "I'll never get used to the miracle of birth. It's the perfect expression of God's magnificence."

Shannon's throat was tight with emotion as the mare rose to her feet. In a few minutes, Princess tried her long wobbly legs without success. Minutes passed, but she couldn't get up and maintain her balance.

"Is something wrong?" Shannon asked worriedly when Ward came out of the stall and stood beside her at the gate.

He shook his head.

"Then why don't you help her up?" Shannon asked him impatiently.

"She'll do it herself when she's ready."

"Are you sure?" How could he just stand there and watch the little creature struggling to get up?

"That's the wonderful thing about letting nature have its way. Everything has perfect timing if we will just keep the faith. If we try to force things, we end up in trouble.''

The way he said it, Shannon wondered if there was more than a surface meaning to his words. Patience, certainly, was not one of her strong suits. She preferred to make things happen, but a few moments later, she realized he had spoken wisely. Princess stood on wobbly legs. Calico moved closer to her and, protecting her with the warmth of her body, she allowed her baby to nurse.

The touching scene brought tears to Shannon's eyes. Never had she experienced such a moving, tender scene.

''I know, it's beautiful.'' Ward's voice was husky, and his eyes were misty.

''Yes, beautiful,'' she echoed softly.

The moment was a precious one, and as Ward looked at Shannon's rapturous expression, he knew with a strange sense of certainty there was no woman in the world with whom he'd rather share it.

Chapter Eight

Ward knew his daughter would never get back to sleep if he woke her up with the good news, so he waited until breakfast to tell her about Princess's arrival.

With a shriek, the little girl left the table with her pigtails flapping as she bounded out of the house. Since Beth had been out to see the new arrival earlier, she laughed, poured herself another cup of coffee and let Ward and Shannon follow the little girl to the stable.

"Isn't she the most gorgeous thing in all the world?" Tara hung over the stall gate, bubbling with excitement as she viewed the perfect baby horse. "Can I pet her?" she asked eagerly.

"Maybe later today," Ward said, his eyes twinkling at his young daughter's enthusiasm. "We want to let mother and baby get used to each other first. Calico is going to be very protective of Princess, and we don't want to make her nervous by getting too close."

"I'm not going to hurt Princess," Tara protested.

"I know that, sweetie, but you'll have to be patient. You'll have plenty of chances to show her how much you love her."

"I'm going to bring her treats every day."

"Not a good idea," Ward warned her gently. "If you do that, she'll expect a treat every time she sees you and she'll develop a bad habit of nipping."

As Shannon listened to his gentle instructions, she was struck by the way he was ready to take the time to talk with his daughter. Even on the rare occasions when Shannon's father wasn't consumed with business, he'd never spent time with her, and there had never been any companionship between them. Not like Ward and his daughter, she thought with undisguised envy. It wasn't as if Ward had time on his hands. Shannon knew he'd been up at dawn, getting his chores out of the way so he could help wherever he was needed during the forest fire.

"Remember, Tara," he said tenderly, "Princess won't learn how to be a perfect little saddle horse for you if you don't train her properly. You'll need to give her water, the right feed and make sure that she has a mineral-and-salt block to lick." He pointed to a hard square brownish cube sitting just inside the gate. "That's like daily vitamins for Princess."

"Well, I can come to see her any time I want, can't I?" Tara protested, unwilling to give up all the fun things about having her own horse.

Ward tugged playfully at one of her pigtails. "I guess a couple of dozen times wouldn't hurt. And maybe tonight you could help me clean out her stall."

Tara clapped her hands and turned to Shannon. "You can help, too, if you want to."

As Ward tried to picture Shannon mucking out a horse stall, he muffled a chuckle. "I think the two of us can manage, honey."

Shannon heard the amusement in his tone, and it spoke volumes about the way he thought about her.

Now she had her answer. Tara's childish invitation and his reaction made it clear that he must be laughing to himself at the very thought of her trying to fit in with his lifestyle. She shouldn't have been surprised. His kindness and attention to her were just a part of his generous heart. He'd been honest about the importance faith in God played in his life. She wasn't anything close to the kind of woman with whom he would be willing to share his life.

Her head came up. "Well, I think I'll head back to the house and help Beth. I should be able to handle some dirty dishes without any problem."

Ouch, thought Ward. She was obviously offended by his quick response to Tara's suggestion. "I was thinking that you might ride out with me to check one of the water troughs before I leave for the Junction," he said quickly.

"I told you I don't ride."

"No, what you said was that you haven't ridden up to now," Ward corrected her, smiling.

"It's easy, Shannon," said Tara. "You don't do anything but sit there. Daddy, she can ride old Betsy and I'll ride Harvey. I'll show you, Shannon. It'll be fun. Okay?"

While common sense warned her about setting herself up to look like a fool, an inner voice asked her what she had to lose. Ward already had pegged her as someone who could never fit into his way of life. "Okay. It sounds like fun." She lied with a straight face.

"Well, I guess that settles that," Ward said, hiding his surprise. He hadn't intended for Tara to come along, but he knew that Shannon would have turned his invitation down flat without his daughter's help. "Come on, ladies. Let's saddle up."

Shannon managed to mount a gentle brown speckled horse with comparable ease, and she was a little surprised to find herself riding between Tara and Ward with some degree of pleasure as the three mounts moved across the ground in a slow walk.

"See? It's fun, isn't it?" Tara said, happily. "But it's more fun if you let the horse gallop."

"Oh, I don't think I'm ready for that," Shannon said quickly and searched Ward's face for reassurance. "This nice easy walk is just fine."

"You'd love racing across the meadow with the wind blowing in your hair. There's a total freedom about it that takes away your breath," he said, and then, seeing her worried expression, he added quickly, "But not on your first lesson. Maybe later."

Maybe later. The words had the ring of a false promise in them. They both knew the moment the main highway was open to traffic and she solved her transportation problem, she'd be gone. All this would only be something that had briefly touched her. She would remember it, of course, but only as a water color memory that would fade in the bustle of her life.

By the time Ward checked the water tanks, and they returned to the stable, Shannon was ready to get back on firm ground.

"Wasn't that fun?" Tara asked. "Maybe we can go riding all by ourselves. Ted can saddle up for us."

"No, Tara," Ward said firmly. "You know better than that. You stay out of the stalls and corrals when I'm not around."

His daughter gave him a pouting frown, but by the time they reached the house, she was smiling again. "Anyway, Shannon and I can find something to do."

When he saw Beth waving at them from the back door, he quickened his step. "What is it?"

"The Red Cross called," she said hurriedly. "They need more shelter for people fleeing from some of the threatened canyons. The school is overloaded, and they are trying to find housing even this far away. I told them we could take two or three small families." She shook her head. "I don't know exactly where we'll put them. Anyway, they'll be here this afternoon."

"We'll manage somehow," Ward assured her.

"Of course, we will," she answered briskly as if there never had been a question about it. Without another word, she disappeared into the kitchen and began making plans for feeding the new arrivals.

Shannon felt a sudden tightening in her stomach. More people. More tension. No longer would the ranch provide peace and quiet. She hated the thought of being engulfed in a mass of frightened strangers, enduring the same kind of crowded, tense atmosphere as at the school. She caught Ward's searching eyes on her, as if he was reading her thoughts and emotions.

"It's going to be all right," he assured her. "We have to try to take care of anyone who needs our help. We can't cross on the other side of the road." Ward knew from her puzzled expression that she missed his reference to the parable of the good Samaritan. Obviously Biblical teachings were not familiar to her, and he was saddened by the great spiritual gulf between them.

Shannon could tell he was disappointed in her response to this latest crisis. Apparently he didn't mind having his home turned into public housing at a moment's notice. An inner voice reminded her that she couldn't very well fault his generosity when she had been a beneficiary of it.

Feeling a little ashamed, she asked, "What do you want me to do?"

"Just help wherever you can. I know Beth will appreciate any suggestions you have for handling our unexpected guests."

"This kind of thing is a little out of my line," Shannon protested. Her privacy had always been important to her. She'd never offered to share her home with anyone, let alone a bunch of total strangers. "I'm afraid you've got the wrong gal."

The lines in his face softened. "Maybe not. Somehow, I sense that you're going to be a great blessing in this situation."

"Blessing?" She looked at him with open astonishment. "What kind of blessing?"

He smiled. "That remains to be seen, doesn't it?"

"Well, you have more confidence in me than I do."

"To tell the truth, I have an idea that just keeping a rein on Tara may earn you a halo."

"I'm not sure I'm up to that challenge," Shannon admitted with a wan smile. "Your daughter seems to have her own ideas about a lot of things."

"I know. And if Tara can show off for some youngsters, she may be hard to hold down." He sobered. "Living on a ranch can be great for kids, but it can hold a lot of dangers, too. Someone will need to look after them."

She stiffened. Was he setting her up to be the unofficial volunteer baby-sitter for all the children? Before she could protest, he gave her that winning smile of his and headed for the telephone.

A little later, he tried to reassure her that there were a lot of nice people in the world. "I wouldn't be surprised if some of them turn out to be close friends."

That'll be the day, she thought. If all of them felt as displaced as she did, the whole atmosphere of the house would take a plunging drop downward.

The next few hours passed in a blur as they readied the house for the arrival of the evacuated families. When they heard the cars coming, Ward, Shannon and Tara went out on the front porch to greet them, but Shannon held back and let Ward and Tara greet the new arrivals pouring out of two vans. She counted four men, three women, a baby, two children and a dog.

"Shannon. Shannon." A childish voice squealed her name.

She was totally unprepared for the little boy and the black-and-white dog who bounded up the porch steps to greet her. "Kenny. Pokey," she gasped.

Kenny gave her a hug around the knees, and Pokey bounded around her, jumping and barking as he demanded his share of attention.

"I don't believe it." Laughing, she hugged Kenny and tried to keep the exuberant pup from knocking her over. "I wasn't expecting to see you."

"The school got too crowded. And my dad said Mr. Dawson asked for us specially."

"He did?" Shannon rounded her eyes in disbelief. How could that be? Ward only knew this morning that they were going to have people coming to the ranch. He must have requested Kenny's family when he returned the call to the evacuation center.

He had done this for her, she was sure of it. Knowing that she was anxious about being surrounded by total strangers again, he was trying to make the situation as pleasant for her as possible. She'd never had anyone look after her or care about her feelings before. She felt totally ashamed of herself.

"Pokey hated that old kennel. Now he can run all over the place. Mama says this will be a much better place for my baby sister, and Grandpa came, too. Isn't that great?"

"Yes," she said huskily. "Just great."

Beth came out of the house with a broad smile of welcome on her face. "So they're here."

Shannon watched her greet everyone as if it would be no trouble at all to furnish room and board for three more families. Tara was ecstatic because there was a little girl, Gloria, about her own age, and the two of them immediately skipped off to Tara's room as if they were longtime friends instead of strangers.

The men carried Grandpa in his wheelchair up the porch steps and settled him in a small room off the kitchen. A double bed had been moved into the front parlor for Mr. and Mrs. Winters, a retired couple in their sixties. Ward gave up his bedroom to Kenny's parents and provided a pad and sleeping bag for Kenny. The guest room Shannon had occupied was given to Gloria's family, with a small air mattress for the little girl. Ward was going to sleep on a cot in the tack room in the stable, and Shannon was to share Beth's bedroom. The gratitude of the three evacuated families made Shannon feel doubly guilty about her earlier dread.

As soon as she had a moment alone with Ward, she said, ''Thank you for inviting Kenny's family to the ranch.''

''Well, I knew that you're very special to them, and it's a good thing to be around people who make you feel good.''

''That was very thoughtful of you. You make me feel ashamed sometimes.''

''I don't want you to feel ashamed, Shannon. What I want you to feel is worthy of love.'' His tender gaze studied her face. ''You are, you know. Shannon, if you don't love yourself, you won't have any to give to someone else.''

''Isn't loving yourself being narcissistic?''

''Selfish love, yes, but not love that comes from knowing you are a beloved child of God. That kind of caring spills out to everyone. I suspect that you've put a tight cap on the well of love within you, but some day it will burst free, and when it does, there'll be some very lucky people standing in that shower.''

The way he was looking at her made her wonder if he was hoping he might be around to see it. Then she chided herself for trying to read something into his kind generosity and general concern.

''I think Reverend Cozzins should be careful about holding onto his job. Have you ever thought about being a preacher?'' she asked with a teasing grin.

He chuckled. ''Nope. But thanks. I don't think anyone else has ever taken me for a man of the cloth. Quite the contrary, in fact. But that's another story.''

''Well, since Beth and I are rooming together, maybe I'll have the chance to hear it from her.''

He made light of the idea but silently wished there had been time for him to tell her himself how he'd come to recognize that all things work to the good of those that love the Lord.

As the wildfire continued into the second week, daily anxiety about the spreading devastation lay heavily on the hearts of the displaced families. The small television in the sitting room kept them abreast of the growing number of acres being lost every day. They collected each evening to pray and listen to Beth read from her well-worn Bible.

Shannon felt at peace during the evening devotions but failed to summon any kind of miraculous conversion. She wished somehow she could tap into Ward's strong faith. He seemed to have enough to uplift everybody in the house.

All the men except Grandpa left the ranch each

morning after chores so they could help out in the threatened areas. The women shared the cooking and household chores with Beth—all but Shannon. As she had suspected, her job was watching the two girls and Kenny.

"She draws great pictures," the little boy told Tara and Gloria as they walked to the stable to check on Calico and Princess.

Tara proudly led the way to Calico's stall. As the three children hung on the stall gate, the little girl gave them an enthusiastic lecture on the caring and raising of young horses. Shannon hid a smile, wishing Ward could have been there to hear his daughter repeat his teachings.

When Tara noticed the water bucket was half empty, she said, "We have to fill it up."

"No, we don't," Shannon said firmly. There was no way she was going to let the little girl open the stall to fill the water bucket or anything else. "Your father will take care of it when he gets home."

"Calico is thirsty," she said, setting her mouth in a stubborn line. "And I know how to carry water to the stalls."

"I'm sure you do. And when your father does the chores tonight, you can help him. There's still plenty of water in the bucket." Shannon ignored her pugnacious scowl.

Kenny wanted to know all about the other horses. "Maybe there's one I could ride," he suggested hopefully.

"I guess old slowpoke Betsy would be all right for you," Tara said, obviously still out of sorts. "Shannon rode her, and she doesn't know anything about horses."

Shannon hid a smile. Obviously, Tara was no longer her champion because she wouldn't let the little girl have her way. When they got to the house, Shannon agreed to draw some pictures for them to color. She sat with the children outside at the picnic table, and she appeased Tara by sketching a young horse in a nearby corral.

"I'll do one of Princess and Calico later on," she promised, secretly pleased at the way she was able to capture the essence of the sleek, graceful Appaloosa.

The afternoon passed pleasantly, but Shannon was relieved when it was time to collect their things and go inside. Kenny and Gloria bounded upstairs, and Tara disappeared into the kitchen. Shannon decided to join the Winterses in the sitting room to watch the latest report on the fire.

As the horrible orange and red inferno blazed on the screen, the thought of Ward being anywhere near the fire line brought a cold sweat into the palms of her hands. Already there had been a tragic loss of life fighting the fire, and she knew that he wouldn't hesitate to put himself in danger. He would be the first to volunteer anywhere they needed him.

Shannon left the older couple watching a game show and was leaving the sitting room when Beth poked her head out of the kitchen. "Have you seen Tara? I sent her out to the garden for some lettuce a half hour ago."

"I'll go check on her."

"Thanks, Shannon. That child can find more ways to dawdle over the simplest task."

When Shannon reached the garden, she didn't see any sign of the little girl. Remembering the stubborn thrust of Tara's chin when she wanted to enter Calico's stall and fill the water container, Shannon was willing to bet the little girl had decided to do it anyway. She must have gone to the stable.

Shannon hurriedly left the garden and headed in that direction.

The door to the stable was ajar, confirming Shannon's suspicion that Tara was there instead of in the garden, as she was supposed to be.

"Tara," she called as she headed down the row of stalls toward Calico's. No answer, nor any sign of the little girl hanging on the stall gate. Maybe she'd been wrong thinking that Tara had run off to see her new horse. Maybe Tara was busy getting water. Shannon wondered if there was an outside pump. The rear door to the stable was closed. She couldn't think where the child might be.

As she approached the half gate, she saw that Calico was standing quietly near the back of her stall with the colt. Everything seemed serene, but when Shannon looked over the gate to see if the water container had been filled, she froze in horror and cried, "Tara!"

The little girl's crumpled body lay unconscious on the floor of the stall. Blood stained the edge of the rocklike mineral and salt block, and Shannon knew with sickening horror that Tara must have lost her balance climbing over the gate, trying to get the water bucket, and had struck her head on the block when she fell.

Chapter Nine

Shannon threw open the stall gate and knelt by the unconscious child, calling her name, but Tara did not respond. There was a frightening whiteness in her face. The horses were still standing quietly at the back of the stall, even though the gate was open. Shannon knew Tara was too heavy for her to carry to the house. Hurriedly, she shut the gate, raced the length of stable and burst out the door, yelling for help as she ran.

Beth heard Shannon's frantic call from the kitchen and ran out of the house. "What's happened? What's the matter?"

"It's Tara. She's hurt."

"Where?"

"In Calico's stall."

The two women ran as fast as they could to the stable, and Beth quickly knelt beside the unconscious child. "Tara, baby. Oh, dear God."

When the little girl didn't respond, Beth picked her

up in her strong arms and rushed out of the stall, yelling at Shannon to shut the gate.

Before Shannon could respond, Calico started moving toward the open gate with the little colt wobbling close beside her. The mare looked enormous coming at her, and Shannon's instinct to get out of the way fought with her determination not to let them out.

"Back, back," Shannon ordered, waving her arms. Calico tossed her head, but she stopped just short of the open gate, and Shannon managed to get it shut.

She raced out of the stable and caught up with Beth.

"We'll have to call 911, and they'll send an ambulance from Elkhorn," Beth said, her face creased with worry. She laid Tara on the living room couch, then raced to the phone while Shannon stayed by the little girl's side.

The emergency operator informed Beth that because of the fire, there was an overload on ambulance services. She wasn't certain that one would be immediately available, but she would alert the authorities to the emergency so they would allow the Dawson vehicle through the Beaver Junction roadblock to Elkhorn. "If there's an ambulance available at the Junction, I'll have them meet you at the roadblock, and they can take the child from there into Elkhorn."

Beth said, "We'll leave immediately. Can you locate Ward Dawson and tell him that we're taking his injured daughter to the hospital?"

"I'll do my best. Good luck."

By this time the whole house was alerted to the emergency, and Kenny's mother insisted they take their new van instead of Beth's old model car. "There's room for the child to lie down in the back. If I didn't have the baby to tend I'd drive you.''

"Shannon can do that," Beth said crisply, and handed her the car keys. "If Ward calls, tell him to get to the Elkhorn hospital as quickly as possible.''

"We'll be holding a prayer vigil for Tara," Mrs. Winters promised. The other two women nodded. As they hurried out of the house, Shannon heard Kenny ask, "God will make her well, won't He?"

Beth sat in the back with Tara, holding her gently but firmly in her arms. The little girl's breathing was raspy, but the bleeding from her head wound had stopped.

Shannon drove the speed limit all the way to Beaver Junction. Her experience driving mountain roads was negligible, and the pressure of precious minutes slipping by brought a cold sweat to her forehead. Her hands had a clammy wetness as they tightly gripped the steering wheel.

She could hear Beth praying over the unconscious child and trying to rouse her with tender and loving murmurs. Shannon wanted to pray, but she wasn't sure that the lines of communication were open between her and any divine spirit. Nevertheless, she found herself praying, "Please let there be an ambulance in Beaver Junction to take Tara to the hospital.''

When they reached the roadblock, Shannon wasn't surprised that her prayer wasn't answered. She really hadn't expected that it would be. She did the best she could to make time on the double-lane highway. Fortunately Beth seemed to know every turn and curve in the road.

When they finally reached the hospital, Shannon was not prepared for the snarl of traffic going in and out. Even the emergency entrance was crowded with vehicles, and scurrying hospital personnel were trying to assess the priorities of those needing attention.

A male intern came out to the van, took one look at Tara and whisked her away into the ER on a stretcher.

Beth and Shannon kept a silent vigil in the midst of organized chaos in the waiting room. It was nearly thirty minutes before a nurse approached them. She glanced uncertainly at Shannon and then Beth. "Who is the mother of the little girl?"

"Her mother is deceased. I'm her aunt," Beth said quickly. "How is she? She's going to be all right, isn't she?"

"The doctor is still doing tests," she replied with practiced calmness. "It may be a couple of hours before they are finished. Is there a father—"

"Yes, my brother. He's a volunteer, helping out some of the firefighters. We've left word for him to come here as soon as possible."

"Good. Try not to worry. We're doing everything we can for your little girl."

She started to turn away, but Beth stopped her. "Is there a chapel?"

"Yes, on the second floor."

"Thank you." Beth rose to her feet, and Shannon didn't know whether to go with her or stay in the waiting room. She didn't want to intrude if Beth wanted to be alone in this moment of crisis.

"Shall I wait for you here?" she asked.

"No." Beth looked surprised at the question, and as

if Shannon's prayers were as important as her own, she added, "This is a time to call upon our Heavenly Father for Tara's healing. I'll leave word at the desk so Ward will know where to find us."

Meekly, Shannon followed Beth into the softly lit small chapel, wondering if someone would challenge her right to be there. A few people sat quietly in the pews, bowing their heads or staring at a simple altar holding two lighted candles.

Beth slipped into one of the pews, then quickly knelt on the knee bench, folding her hands as her lips began to move in prayer.

Shannon sat stiffly in the pew, her eyes fixed on some unseen point in front of her. She knew Beth expected her to pray, but she didn't know any of the right words. Fear and anxiety dominated her thoughts. Why had this happened? Ward had trusted her to watch his daughter. And she had failed him. If Tara didn't recover, it would be her fault. How could she ever live with herself? She wanted to run away and hide.

When they left the chapel and returned to the waiting room, there still was no news about Tara's condition. Beth couldn't sit still. "I'm going to see if I can find the cafeteria and get a cup of coffee."

"I'll stay here just in case they tell us something," Shannon said, her stomach in knots from the long hours of waiting. She covered her face with her hands, and silent tears streamed down her face.

When someone gently pulled her hands away from her face, she stared in disbelief. "Ward!" With a whimper, she turned and buried her face in his shoulder. "I'm sorry...I'm so sorry."

"How is she?"

"They haven't told us anything," she said tearfully.

"Where's Beth?"

"She went for coffee." Shannon pulled away and faced him. "It's all my fault. She wanted to fill the water bucket, and I wouldn't let her. Calico still had water, and I didn't think it was important to get her any more. I told her to wait until you got home." She'd turned a deaf ear to the child's concern, and with her stubborn willfulness, Tara had decided to take care of the matter herself.

Ward brushed a lock of hair on Shannon's forehead. "Then it's not your fault. That was the right thing to tell her. Tara knows she's not to open any stall—"

"She didn't." Shannon's lower lip trembled. "Tara must have been climbing over the gate to get the water bucket and lost her balance. There was blood on the mineral block. Oh, Ward, what'll we do?"

Ward didn't answer her, but bowed his head. From the moment he'd learned about his daughter's accident, prayers for her well-being had been on his lips and in his heart. Quietly, he prayed, "Father, You have all the power in heaven and earth, and I know that when I call upon Your name, You hear me. I ask that You touch Tara with Your healing power, and I know that You will because You have promised that all things are possible to those who believe. She is in Your hands, Lord, and I thank You for Your loving kindness. Amen."

Shannon remained silent, and when Beth came back, she asked Ward if he would like to spend a few minutes in the chapel. He nodded, and Beth told him where it was located. He glanced at Shannon, silently asking if she wanted to accompany him, but she shook her head.

It was another hour before a nurse led the three of them into a private consultation office. A middle-aged doctor with thinning sandy-colored hair and gold-rimmed spectacles turned and introduced himself. "I'm Dr. McGrail."

Ward quickly introduced himself. "I'm Tara's father. This is my sister, Beth, and this is Shannon Hensley, a friend of the family."

The doctor acknowledged the introductions and motioned to some chairs in front of a desk. "Please have a seat." Then he sat down and picked up some papers. "I know that you're anxious to hear what our tests have shown about your little girl's injury. We've done a CT scan and a complete battery of X rays."

He paused for a moment, and Shannon's heart lunged in her throat. Then he gave them a faint smile. "Under the circumstances, the news is good. She has suffered a concussion, but there is no internal bleeding. We are hopeful that the swelling caused by the blow will recede without any complications."

There was a moment of breathless silence, and then Beth said, prayerfully, "Thank you, dear Lord."

"Amen," echoed Ward, letting out a deep breath of relief. "She's going to be okay." Unexpectedly, he took Shannon's hand and squeezed it.

"Your daughter has regained consciousness, and you may see her, Mr. Dawson, but only for a few minutes. We'll keep her in intensive care overnight. A family member may visit for five minutes every hour. Tomorrow we'll see about moving her to a private room."

Shannon knew that Beth was disappointed not to be allowed in the ICU for the first visit, but as they waited for Ward to see Tara, the lines in Beth's face eased.

"We need to call home and thank everyone for their prayers." Then she hugged Shannon. "If you hadn't found her when you did and driven us here so quickly through all that traffic mess, she might have been a lot worse."

Shannon's feelings of guilt overrode Beth's expression of gratitude. None of this would have happened if she hadn't ignored Tara's strong feelings.

When Ward came back, the lines in his face had eased. "She's alert and asking questions. I told her as much as I knew about what had happened. She asked about you, Shannon. She seems worried that you're going to be mad at her."

The pain in Shannon's eyes and sad face touched him, and Ward would have drawn her close if Beth hadn't been there. He regretted that she lacked the faith and the spiritual strength to call upon the Lord in a time like this. He wanted to assure her that God had answered his prayers and share with her the thanksgiving that was in his heart. It saddened him to know that even in this crisis, they didn't share a common gratitude for the heavenly Father's blessings. The situation had highlighted more than ever how far apart they were in ways that mattered to him most.

Shannon saw the regret in his expression and knew she had failed to measure up. He had wanted her to go with him to the chapel and pray with him. Her unbelief obviously weighed heavily on him, and she wished things were different between them. She knew that her lack of faith had not only disappointed him, but had made it clear that he would never commit himself to any kind of serious bond between them.

"What are we going to do about all those people at our house?" Beth asked.

Now that the crisis seemed to be over, Beth had started worrying about the stranded families. Her care-taking nature immediately shifted into high gear.

"They'll take care of themselves," Ward reassured his sister. "And Ted will tend to the chores. It's better that we wait and see how Tara is in the morning. No use all three of us staying here at the hospital all night, though. I'll make some calls and see if I can find a motel room. With all the extra people in town because of the fires, we may be out of luck."

His words were prophetic. There wasn't an empty room to be found. Ward was resigned that all three of them would be spending the night in the waiting room when a middle-aged woman who seemed familiar approached him. She was wearing a volunteer smock and badge.

"Aren't you Ward Dawson?" She held out her hand. "I'm Sue Williams. You probably don't remember me, I'm Laura Cozzins's sister. I was widowed a couple of years ago, and I've seen you at church a couple of times when I was visiting. Do you have someone in the hospital?"

Ward explained the situation. After a short conversation, and a generous offer from Sue Williams, Shannon and Beth left to spend the night at the widow's spacious home. Ward would be keeping the vigil at the hospital.

Thankful that Christian charity had answered their needs, Ward settled himself in the waiting room, glad to be able to make short visits to the ICU to hold his daughter's hand while she slept.

Shannon had wanted to be alone with him before leaving, but there hadn't been an opportunity. A friend of the family was all she was in this situation, and she left the hospital with Beth, feeling displaced and empty.

"I'll be home after my shift ends," Sue had told them. "Here's the address and a key to the front door."

They drove to the address the widow had given them and gratefully accepted her hospitality.

In spite of Shannon's physical and emotional exhaustion, she spent a restless night in a strange bed and borrowed nightgown. In a chilling nightmare, the distance between Ward and herself stretched and stretched until she couldn't see him anymore. When Ward's accusing voice resounded in her ears, she awoke with a cry and his name on her lips.

As she lay there, feeling emotionally depleted and empty, she realized for the first time how much his approval had come to mean to her, an approval that she would never have.

By the time she'd showered and dressed in the wrinkled outfit of the day before, she had decided to take charge of her life the only way she knew how—making her own decisions and carrying them out by herself. Now that she was in Elkhorn, she would find a way to leave the area. There was nothing to keep her there. Her growing feelings for Ward were a mockery of the truth that even though he liked her and might be attracted to her, he was committed to a strong religious faith that she couldn't share. The regretful way he had looked at her last night had spoken volumes. There was no reason for her to return to the ranch. No reason at all.

She pleaded a headache and let Beth and Mrs. Williams go to the hospital without her. Then she put a ten-dollar bill under the bedroom phone and made a couple of long distance calls. The first was to the Los Angles employment agency.

"Oh, I'm so glad you called, Miss Hensley," the woman said with obvious relief. "You really should have kept in close touch with us. Good news. We've lined up two very promising interviews for you, and if you will give me the date of your return, I'll schedule them."

When she mentioned the names of the companies, Shannon felt a quiver of excitement and answered firmly. "I'm sure that I can make arrangements to be in Los Angles within the week, but I'll have to let you know for sure."

She hung up and immediately called her bank. The money on her rented apartment had come in. Her finances had improved, and she had the option of using her credit cards to get to Los Angeles.

When the doorbell rang, Shannon hurried downstairs to open the door, ready to say that Mrs. Williams wasn't home. Her breath suddenly caught when she saw Ward standing there.

"Good morning," he said, a weak smile on his tired, unshaven face. "How's the headache?"

"It's better," she said, remembering in time the excuse she'd given for not going to the hospital. "You don't look so good. How's Tara?"

"She made it through the night in good shape." He rubbed his eyes as if struggling to keep them open. "They'll be doing more tests this morning. I thought I'd catch a couple hours sleep while Beth takes over."

"I'll show you where you can crash." As they walked up the stairs together, he smiled at her, and she let herself enjoy his masculine closeness. Nothing about him brought out her fierce competitive nature or distrust. It was a unique experience for her, and one she would not soon forget.

She showed him the bedroom where she had slept. She hadn't gotten around to stripping the sheets from her bed like a good houseguest, and it was obvious from the rumpled covers that she'd had a bad night. She smoothed them as quickly as she could.

"The bathroom is across the hall. Have a nice sleep." She paused in the doorway, wanting to tell him about her decision to fly to Los Angles as soon as possible, but the weary slump of his shoulders held her back. She'd tell him when he woke up.

"Shannon, wait a minute. You aren't still blaming yourself for all of this, are you?"

She avoided answering his question. "Can't we talk about this later?"

The way she caught her lower lip and avoided looking at him was answer enough for Ward. If he hadn't been so blasted tired, he would have settled the matter right then and there. Later he realized he shouldn't have let the moment pass without confronting her sense of guilt.

While he slept, Shannon skimmed through the yellow pages of the telephone directory and began her search for transportation that would get her to Denver's international airport. Buying a car and driving to Los Angeles was out of the question. The lack of daily bus and train service to the small mountain community and her limited funds narrowed her options considerably. An expensive shuttle service that made a daily run into Denver seemed to be her best bet. If she imposed on Mrs. Williams one more night, she could use her credit card and make a reservation on a red-eye flight to Los Angeles the next night.

She was on the phone most of the morning, sitting at a kitchen counter making her calls. She had just hung up from talking to the employment agency again when she realized Ward had come into the room. One look at his questioning expression told her he'd overheard her discussing her plans.

"You're leaving?" Ward asked with a stab of disbelief. She couldn't go. Not yet. He'd seen a marked change in her in the few days that she'd been at the school and ranch, a softening of her defenses, a growing willingness to allow other people into her life. He'd been encouraged that with a little more time to find herself, she'd experience the right relationship with the Lord.

"I'm going tomorrow," she told him. "I've found transportation to Denver."

He eased down on a stool beside her and resisted the temptation to reach over and take her hand in a gesture of persuasion. "Why do you have to go? Why can't you stay?"

The answer was so simple, she wondered why he had to ask. "Because I don't belong here."

"Maybe you would if you didn't rush off like this."

"Stay and cause everyone more trouble? No, thank you. If I had only helped Tara with refilling a simple bucket of water for the horses, none of this would have happened."

"And you didn't help her because?"

"Because I don't know anything about taking care of horses," she answered defensively. "And I was trying not to do anything wrong or stupid."

"Doesn't that seem like a pretty good reason to refuse her? You were being cautious and had no reason to think Tara would sneak back and do something so foolish and dangerous."

She shook her head.

"I saw that she was concerned about Princess, and I turned a deaf ear to her. You asked me to look after your daughter, and I let you down, pure and simple."

"Is this why you're leaving? You believe all of us are blaming you? And you're running away?"

"That's part of it," she admitted. "But it's time I got my life back. At the moment I don't know what's going to happen or if I'm going to be able to handle all the challenges, but the sooner I start, the better. I can't stay here."

He searched her deepening gray-blue eyes. "Why not?"

"Because...because..." Because I'm in love with you. In horror, she wondered if she had spoken the words aloud. They seemed to come from nowhere. Clear. Honest. Shattering. In spite of herself, she'd fallen in love with a man who lived the convictions of his heart. He had made it clear what kind of a woman he wanted to share his life. And it wasn't her.

"Are you running away from me? Yourself?" God?

Her chest was suddenly tight as she slipped off her stool and walked to a kitchen counter where Mrs. Williams had left a pot of coffee brewing. With trembling hands she took down two cups and filled them.

"Are you hungry? I can see what's in the fridge. You'll need to eat something before you go back to the hospital."

When his warm breath brushed her neck, she knew he had come up behind her. She stiffened, not wanting to turn and look into those arresting eyes of his or be tempted by the inviting curve of his lips. She needed to put some distance between them before she made a fool of herself.

"What is it, Shannon? Why are you running away?" he asked quietly, as he put his hands on her shoulders and gently turned her.

Her chin came up. "I'm not running away. I've got to get back to Los Angeles. It's time, don't you think?" she said with a rueful smile. "I've lost my car and all my belongings." And my heart.

"Maybe you haven't lost as much as you think. There may be a hidden blessing in all of this that you're overlooking."

"I don't know what it could be." After tomorrow she would probably never see him again. The memories she would be taking back to the city would only make her aware of being alone and rejected. "I really can't wait to put this all behind me," she lied. "I hope I can see Tara before I go."

"The doctor said they would probably be moving her into a private room later today."

"I want to stop at the hospital gift shop and buy her something to remember me by."

"I don't think any of us will need a reminder of your time with us," he said, trying to still a silent rebellion in his heart. He didn't want to let her go. If there had been any argument that would have convinced her to stay, he might have been tempted to use it. Only a deeply rooted belief that the matter was out of his hands, and in God's, kept him silent.

Chapter Ten

Beth called Ward from the hospital to tell him that Tara's morning tests had been positive and that they were going to move her to a private room after lunch.

"The doctor wants to keep her twenty-four hours for observation. He confessed that he'd never seen someone recover so quickly from such a hard bump on the head. I just smiled. The Bible tells us that it is done unto us as we believe. We believed that God would work a miracle for us, and He did. Tara is sleeping now, and I was thinking that you might want to do the shopping and pick up the supplies we need before you come back to the hospital. Maybe by then she'll be out of ICU and in her own room."

"Yes, that sounds like a good idea. That list you gave me will likely fill up the whole back of the pickup," he teased, and added, "Shannon will probably want to pick up a few things for her trip. She's leaving for Denver tomorrow."

"Tomorrow," Beth echoed. "You mean she's not going back to the ranch?"

He tried to ignore the dead feeling in his chest. "Shannon's made arrangements to catch a flight to Los Angeles, but I'm sure she'll want to say goodbye to you and Tara."

Beth sighed. "Maybe it's for the best, Ward. I don't want you hurt, and anyone around the two of you for two minutes can see how you feel about her. I know what you were hoping, we both were, but you can't make someone change just because you want them to. Oh, maybe on the surface, but not deep down. They have to find the Lord themselves."

"I know." Ward didn't need his sister to tell him how difficult it was to change and find a relationship with God. He'd been there himself.

After he hung up the kitchen phone, he turned to Shannon, who was still sitting at the counter. "I need to pick up some supplies for Beth and stop by the vet's to get some medicine for one of my horses. Was I right in telling Beth you might want to stop in town?"

She nodded. "I'm down to the clothes on my back and the personal items in my purse. I'll want to stop at a bank and use my ATM card." She was thankful that the rent money had come in the nick of time to get her back to California.

"All right, let's go. I'll show you the bustling town of Elkhorn." Now that the hours in Shannon's company were numbered, Ward intended to spend as many of them with her as he could.

"What about your breakfast? All you've had is toast

and coffee.'' She knew he was used to the big break-
fasts Beth prepared every morning.

''We'll stop somewhere. It's almost time for lunch,
anyway. Somehow I don't feel like a crowded café. Is
fast-food all right by you?''

''Fine.''

They took his pickup and headed toward the business district. Ward obviously knew his way around
town and pointed out some interesting landmarks.
When he pulled up to a drive-through window at a
popular fast-food place and they gave their orders,
Shannon expected to eat in the car, but he surprised
her by driving away from the parking lot.

''There are some picnic tables in a small park down
by the river. Let's take our lunch and eat there.''

A picnic? Today of all days?

''Is that okay?'' he asked, seeing her surprise.

''Yes, fine.'' He never ceased to surprise her. No
matter what the world threw at him, he seemed to find
ways to make life a pleasure instead of something to
be endured. She was envious of the quiet corner within
him that remained sure and unchanging and was
amazed at how being with him eased the tension that
had been building all morning.

''Here we are,'' he said as he turned into a parking
space that bordered a small park close to a wide, slow-
moving river. Several picnic tables were scattered under huge oak trees, and they walked down a grassy
slope to one near the river. ''I like being near moving
water.''

''I know,'' she said, and her chest was suddenly tight

as she remembered the day he had picked her up in his arms and carried her across the mountain stream.

"It's great fun rafting on this river," he told her as they ate, entertaining her with stories about riding rubber tubes down the river and fishing along its banks. As he talked, Shannon smiled, picturing the energetic and adventuresome boy who had probably sat under this very tree many times. Maybe he'd even brought a teenage sweetheart here to sit and watch the water while they held hands or stole an adolescent kiss. In one way, she wanted to ask him about the girls and women who'd been a part of his life, but in another way, she didn't want to know.

"Laura told me you'd been a handful when you were growing up," Shannon said, wanting to keep him talking about himself and all the things that made him who he was.

He laughed, a deep rich sound that she'd come to love.

"I guess there are plenty of folks around who'll bear witness to that, all right. In a way you get your just desserts when you spend your life around people who knew you when. Just this morning I ran into Samuel Shornberger when I was putting gas in the truck." He chuckled. "I could tell from his frosty greeting that he hasn't forgotten me after all these years."

"And who is Samuel Shornberger?"

"He was an Elkhorn high school coach when I was a student there. Before they built the consolidated school at Beaver Junction, we were bused into Elkhorn for high school. We didn't have much of a football team, and Coach Shornberger wasn't exactly on any of the players' good fellow list. One time a couple of us managed to get hold of a pair of red sweatpants he always wore, and we hooked them to the flagpole so the next morning when he drove up, they were flying over the school as pretty as you please.''

Shannon laughed with him, visualizing the prank and wishing her school days had been filled with friends and fun times. She had missed all that. This moment of sharing created a poignant longing in her for what might have been if they'd met earlier. She shoved the fantasy aside. What was, was.

Ward watched the laughter fade from her lips and eyes, and as dappled sunlight moved over her fair hair, touching the sweet lines of her face, he couldn't stop himself from asking, "Why don't you stay a little longer, Shannon?"

"I can't. I've got to get my life back on track as soon as possible. I'll be interviewing for a couple of positions with companies that will give me a chance for advancement."

As she talked about the prospect of new employment, he was reminded of the first time he'd met her. Even then he'd glimpsed a softness under that brisk demeanor. He silently sighed. If only there were more time to show her a different way of life than the one she knew. He was certain she would be successful in securing the kind of position she wanted, and the vulnerable part of her that needed love would once again be deeply buried in the world's pressures. He had prayed for her, for himself and for guidance and he knew there was nothing he could do now but let go, and let God.

Sighing, he glanced at his watch. "Well, I guess we better get a move on. While you go to the bank and do your shopping, I'll stop at the vet's and feed store."

"All right. It won't take me long." Shannon had already decided on the few things she needed to buy. She'd asked Ward to mail her the items she'd left at the ranch. "Will you be going back to the ranch tonight?" she asked, hoping he would say no. If he stayed in town, they might have some time together. Now that time was short, she was guilty of wanting to delay their parting for as long as possible.

"If Tara is doing okay, I really have to get back. Ted needs help keeping everything going at the ranch, and I don't know how soon my other ranch hands will be free from their volunteer duties. This wildfire has played heck with everyone's life."

"Hasn't it?" she replied dryly as she nodded in agreement.

"I was gone all day yesterday, and I'll need to run these supplies home," he told her, reluctantly. "Beth can stay with Tara until she's released, and then I'll come back. We'll caravan to the ranch."

Shannon shoved away a tinge of guilt about leaving, telling herself there was no need for her to stick around. Tara was in good hands. The little girl had a loving family to take care of her. Shannon decided she'd be more in the way than anything.

They finished their lunch and gathered the trash. Ward suggested, "Why don't we meet at the grocery store and you can help me shop for the things Beth wants?"

"You might be better off by yourself," Shannon

warned with a smile. "Buying groceries for one person doesn't exactly provide a lot of experience in wise shopping."

Ward grinned. "Well, then, I'll just have to put the blame on you if I get the wrong brand or size this time."

"Maybe it's a good thing I won't be there when you unload them at the ranch," she said, trying for the same light tone.

"Yes, you'll be gone," he said quietly, his smile fading. The truth of the words created a strained silence as they walked to the pickup.

Everything went smoothly at the bank, and Shannon breathed a sigh of relief as she left the building with money in her pocket. Using her charge card, she made several purchases at a nearby boutique, including a small suitcase. She chose a pair of tailored mint-green slacks, a short-sleeve blouse and a matching summer jacket for traveling. In addition to a nightgown and short robe, she bought several sets of lingerie. Weary of her limited wardrobe, Shannon had expected to feel good about having something new to wear, but she didn't. She left the store with numerous packages but with little joy.

Every place she went people were talking about the forest wildfire, and televisions were tuned to the latest news—which wasn't good. Thousands of acres had already been burned, and every time the fighters put out one hot spot, another would develop. The weather forecast was the worst, dry and windy.

Shannon wished she could get on a plane that very moment and get away. It would be a relief to get back into her old reassuring patterns. Even though her life was extremely stressful at times, she'd proven that she was capable of handling demanding responsibilities and holding her own in the corporate world. Ever since she'd become a refugee from the forest wildfire, she had lost the security of being in command. She was tired of feeling off balance, adrift and confronted with challenges that seemed to have no solutions. Admitting to herself how she felt about Ward only compounded the need to leave as soon as possible.

His pickup was already in the parking lot of the supermarket when she got there. It took her a few minutes, wandering through different aisles, before she found him at the meat counter. His grocery basket had some meat packages in it, and he was staring at his list with such a furrowed brow that Shannon had to smile.

"Problems?"

He pointed at a couple of hastily written words. "What does that say? I can read pork chops, but not the other words."

"Herb stuffing. Apparently Beth is going to bake some stuffed pork chops."

"Oh." His brow smoothed. "Thanks. Where do we find herb stuffing?"

She laughed. "We hunt. Every grocery store is different."

Walking beside Ward as he pushed the cart, Shannon checked Beth's list and read the posted signs hanging from the ceiling. Finding the exact item and brand became kind of a treasure hunt as they went from one end of the store to the other.

"I found it." Ward triumphantly held up a particular

brand of starch that had been shelved in an inconspicuous place.

Shannon wasn't aware of anyone noticing their laughter and amusement until one woman customer said enviously, "I wish I could get my husband to have that much fun shopping with me."

Husband. Shannon was too startled to correct her, but the fun she'd been having suddenly left. Ward was not her husband. He would never be her husband. She was glad he hadn't heard the remark, and when he came back to the cart, she asked rather curtly, "Are we about through?"

The change in her voice and expression startled him. He gave her a quick look. "What's the matter?"

"Nothing."

"Something has upset you," he insisted. "What?"

She pretended to rearrange the crowded grocery cart while she got her feelings under control. Then she looked up and said evenly, "People are getting the wrong impression, seeing us shopping together. They think we're a couple. You may have a lot of explaining to do when this gets on the grapevine."

"And that should worry me?" He frowned. "Why?"

"Because we're not a couple. We never will be." She faced him steadily. "In less than twenty-four hours I'll be gone. And whatever might have been between us will be another casualty of a Colorado forest fire."

"It doesn't have to be that way," he argued. "Lots of things take time and patience."

"I know what you're hoping—that I'll change. But the truth is, I can't help but be skeptical about the

Christian beliefs that are so important to you. I've never experienced anything in my life that makes me think there's a Supreme Being the least bit interested in me. I can't pretend to be something I'm not.''

"Why are you so ready to shut down on yourself—and me?"

"Because I know what I want out of life. Success. Freedom. Independence." She squared her shoulders.

"Really? Are you trying to convince me or yourself?"

"There are a lot more important things than love."

Ward didn't believe for one minute that she spoke the truth that was in her heart. If there was anyone who desperately needed to be nurtured, loved and cared for it was Shannon Hensley. That brisk, I-don't-need-anyone veneer of hers didn't fool him. "Why don't you quit lying to yourself?" he asked gently.

She turned away without giving him an answer. They returned to the pickup in silence. On the drive to the hospital, she was defensive and rigid on her side of the seat. Finally, he decided to speak his mind. This might be the last time they would be alone together.

"I know this experience has been rough on you, and it's made you angry and frightened, but if you were honest with yourself, you might find that all in all, you've grown in this experience. It's been good for you."

"How can you say that?" She looked at him in utter amazement.

"Whenever something happens that causes us to change and grow, it's for our own good. That's what this earth school is all about, Shannon," he explained patiently. "We are put here to learn and discover the divine nature in each of us. You may think you are the same person you were before this experience, but you're not. You've grown a lot. Just look at the way working with the children has made you a gentler person. Look at the way your creative talent has brought new pleasure."

She choked back an angry reply. And look at the way falling in love with you has brought new misery into my life. He might think she had lowered her defenses against being hurt by him or anyone else, but he was wrong. She hadn't changed. More than ever she felt alone, vulnerable and unwanted. The whole experience had reinforced what she already knew. Life was one long, heartbreaking challenge.

Ward saw her closed expression and was saddened by the truth.

There are none so blind that will not see, and none so deaf that will not hear.

When they arrived at the hospital, they were told that Tara was just being moved to a private room and they would have to wait until the nurses were finished getting her settled.

"I want to stop at the gift shop, anyway," Shannon told Ward.

"Okay, I'll go ahead and find Beth. If I know my sister, she's probably waiting in the chapel."

As Shannon watched him walk down the corridor in that easy, confident way of his, an overwhelming sense of loss created a tightening in her chest. She leaned against a wall, struggling with a wave of emotion that made her breath short.

"Are you all right?" asked a young woman in a volunteer's uniform who was passing with a cart loaded with flowers and books.

"Yes...I'm fine," Shannon stammered.

"You look a little peaked."

"Just something I ate," Shannon lied, feeling foolish. She gave the young woman a false smile. "Where's the gift shop?"

The volunteer motioned in the direction from which she had come. "Just around the corner."

"Thank you." Shannon waited for a moment until the weak sensation in her legs passed, then she walked slowly down the corridor. She was bewildered by the strong physical reaction she'd had watching Ward disappear from sight. What on earth was the matter with her? She felt as if she were perched on a precipice, about to fall off.

By the time she reached the gift shop, she was in control again. The physical and emotional upheaval had passed, her breathing was steady, and she chided herself for giving way to such feminine hysterics.

The gift shop was small, and the choices were limited, but she found a Dr. Seuss book for Tara and a large stuffed Cat In The Hat to match. She was sure the little girl would enjoy having her daddy read the book to her while she hugged the silly happy cat.

Her arms filled with the floppy stuffed toy, she made her way to the second floor, where Ward and Beth were waiting.

"What on earth have you got there?" Ward asked, chuckling, when he saw her.

"It's a cat," she answered, showing them the long-legged creature with the sloppy smile and tall black-and-white hat.

Beth laughed. "Not like any cat I've ever seen."

Shannon replied a little defensively, "Well, I think Tara will like it, and there's a book to go with it."

"I think it's great," Ward assured her, loving the way her cool professionalism gave way at times to an appealing, innocent, girlish charm. The way she was holding the stuffed animal hinted at an early childhood void of such comforting toys. He knew his daughter would treasure the gift because it came from Shannon. She had captured his daughter's heart as deeply as his own, and he wondered how he was going to explain Shannon's disappearance from their lives.

"*Our* little girl is doing wonderfully," Beth told Shannon. "They expect to release her tomorrow."

Our little girl. The possessive noun only highlighted the sudden emptiness Shannon felt, knowing she was going to miss Tara's childish exuberance and love of life.

Dr. McGrail stopped at the waiting room and verified that they could take Tara home in the morning. "She's one spunky little girl," he said, smiling. "I'd keep her off a horse for a week or two, but I don't see any problems ahead."

"Bless you, Doctor, for all that you did," Beth told him gratefully.

"I did very little besides watch a healing take place that went beyond our expectations," he said honestly.

"Somebody up there is watching out for her, that's for sure."

"Yes, and we're grateful to the Lord," Ward said readily.

"Well, your little girl is waiting to see you." The doctor smiled. "She's a talker, that one."

Ward laughed. Tara must be back to normal if she was entertaining everyone with her usual nonstop chatter.

Shannon hesitated about going into the room with Ward and Beth. "Maybe she shouldn't have this much company all at once. I can wait until later."

"No, she'll want to see you." Ward declared and put a guiding hand on her arm. A nurse was leaving as they entered, and she warned, "Don't stay too long."

"Hi, sweetness," Ward greeted Tara as he went to her bed. "Are you ready for company?"

She laughed and held up her arms for a hug and a kiss from her daddy. Shannon's breath caught when she saw how tiny and fragile the little girl looked in the hospital bed. A small bandage clung to the left side of her small head, and a section of her hair had been shaved.

When Tara saw Shannon standing near the foot of the bed, she grinned, and her bright eyes widened when she saw what Shannon had in her arms.

"Is that for me?" she squealed.

"No, it's for me," Ward teased. "But I'll let you play with him once in a while."

Shannon moved to the side of the bed and put the

stuffed toy in Tara's arms. "This is the Cat in the Hat, and here's a book to tell you all about him."

"Thank you," the little girl said, hugging the toy.

"You're very welcome," Shannon said and placed a kiss on Tara's forehead. The child's skin felt soft and sweet under her lips, and when Tara's arms went around her neck in a hug, Shannon blinked back some unexpected tears. She quickly stepped to the foot of the bed.

As she watched Ward smooth his daughter's hair away from her cheek and pat her shoulder lovingly, she fought a sudden urge to flee from the room. That peculiar weakness and tightness in her chest was back again. She must have made some kind of sound, because Ward turned and looked at her.

"Are you all right?" he asked, frowning. She looked pale and had a hand pressed against her chest. "What's the matter? Are you sick?"

She tried for a light laugh. "Of course not."

Ward quickly moved a chair to one side of the bed for her. "Come sit down. You look a little tired."

"When we get home, Shannon, we can read my book," Tara said happily. "And you can draw the silly old cat doing all kinds of crazy things. It'll be fun. I bet Kenny and Gloria have been missing us."

Ward and Beth exchanged glances as they waited for Shannon to tell Tara that she wouldn't be going back to the ranch. When she sent a beseeching glance at him, he ignored her silent plea that he do the explaining. He was afraid the words would catch in his throat.

Shannon swallowed hard. "Tara, honey, I won't be going back to the ranch."

Tara's little face instantly clouded, and she burst into tears. "I'm sorry. I'm sorry I was bad. Please, Shannon, don't go. I'll behave. I'll never, never do anything bad again. I promise. I promise. You can't go," she sobbed. "Please don't go."

"Honey, you don't understand." Shannon quickly stood up and gathered the little girl in her arms, horrified that the child thought she was to blame for Shannon's decision to leave. "Please don't cry. You haven't done anything wrong. You're a wonderful, beautiful little girl, and I love you."

Tara pressed her wet cheek against Shannon's. "You do? And I love you, too." She gulped. "And so does Daddy. And Aunt Beth. And Kenny, and—" She hesitated as she raised her tear-streaked face to Shannon. "Maybe even Calico and Princess. I could show you how to ride better, so you won't bounce all over the place like a city dude."

Ward chuckled. "How can you refuse an offer like that, Shannon?"

"I guess I can't," she answered slowly as she realized why she was feeling ill. Even though it didn't make sense to prolong the inevitable, something deep inside was telling her to delay her return to California. She couldn't get on with her life until she was free of the loving claims a persuasive little girl and her handsome father had put on her.

Chapter Eleven

When Shannon and Beth drove Tara to the ranch the next afternoon, a large paper banner with childish printing was hung over the front door. Welcome Home, Tara.

The little girl clapped her hands when Shannon read it to her.

Kenny and Gloria rushed out of the house ahead of the adults and circled Tara as she got out of the car.

"Oh, no, they shaved part of your head," Gloria wailed.

"Did it get bashed in?" Kenny asked, peering at the bandage with large curious eyes.

Beth opened her mouth to halt the flood of questions, but Tara, obviously pleased by all the attention, began weaving a tale that skirted the truth enough to make her stay in the hospital sound like an exciting adventure.

Ward arrived a few minutes later, having followed

them in the pickup. He expected to find his daughter upstairs in her bed, and he frowned when he saw that Tara had gathered all the well-wishers around her and set up court in the sitting room.

"You should be resting, young lady."

"Daddy—"

"No argument." He picked her up in his arms and passed Beth and Shannon without a glance.

His sister shrugged. "Well, I have work to do."

She disappeared into the kitchen with the three women guests, and Kenny and Gloria raced off to finish a game of horseshoes they'd been playing. Kenny's grandfather wheeled to his room for a nap, and Shannon was left alone in the sitting room.

What am I doing here?

Restless, she walked to the window and stared at a dark swath of smoke swirling above the wooded mountains cupping the valley. By now she could have been on a shuttle bus to Denver, putting a widening distance between her and this whole nightmare. The feelings that had accompanied her decision to return were gone. She couldn't remember why she thought Tara needed her or why she wanted to bring more pain into her life by spending time with Ward. His life was full with his daughter and his horses, and she had little to offer him on any level. If he'd been serious about any kind of a commitment between them, he would have spoken up before now. She'd sabotaged her future by failing to honor the interviews that had been set up for her, and for what?

When Ward came down from Tara's room, he didn't see Shannon and asked Beth where she was.

"Maybe upstairs," his sister answered uncertainly. "I told her we didn't need any help in the kitchen."

"I think she said that she was going for a walk," offered Kenny's mother, who was busy fixing a bottle for the baby.

"Did she take Kenny and Gloria with her?"

"No. They're still playing horseshoes. Gloria's mother is watching them."

"So she went alone?"

Beth chided her brother. "Shannon's a big girl. She can take care of herself."

"In the city, maybe, but she doesn't know beans about rough country like this."

"She'll learn quick enough if she sticks around awhile." She eyed her brother as if asking, Is she sticking around?

Ward ignored the unanswered question, mainly because he didn't know the answer. He didn't know what had happened to Shannon in that hospital room to make her change her mind. Why had she put aside her plans to return to a situation that had challenged her in every possible way? Was it divine guidance that had kept her in his life?

As he left the house by the back door, he let his gaze rove over the open meadow where they had walked under the stars, but he didn't see her small figure anywhere in the wide expanse of wild grasses. Maybe she was walking around the corrals, looking at the horses who were being groomed for sale, or had gone to the stable to see how Calico and Princess were doing.

He asked the two ranch hands who had shown up

for a couple days work if they'd seen her, but they shook their heads.

"No, boss. We've been busy unloading the pickup. We'll keep an eye out and tell her you're looking for her." They exchanged glances as if Ted had already filled them in on the news that the boss had a pretty lady on his mind.

If Shannon wasn't in the meadow, around the corrals or in the stable, where had she gone? The only hike they'd taken together was down to the stream. He stopped short. She wouldn't hike through the thick stands of aspen and pines trying to find her way to the stream, would she? He knew the answer even as the question crossed his mind. Shannon would do anything she put her mind to. Getting lost in the thick stand of timber between here and the stream would be easy for someone who didn't know the way. What if she tried to cross the stream by herself? Or got hurt trying to find her way down some of the rocky bluffs that bordered the water?

These thoughts quickened his long stride, and he began calling her name when he reached the dense forest edging the far pasture, but his voice was swallowed up in the infinity of tree trunks and heavy vegetation. The path was almost invisible, and there were a hundred places where the rising and falling ground would challenge the most seasoned hiker.

He was angry that she would put herself in danger. What was she trying to prove? When he heard the muffled sound of the stream, he rushed forward, breaking through a band of trees and rocks edging the water.

For a minute his eyes didn't register the black-and-white dog who came splashing out of the water with a stick in his mouth.

Then he heard Shannon squeal and saw her sitting on the ground, trying to ward off the dripping wet dog who was determined to deposit the stick in her lap.

"Pokey, no." Laughing, she grabbed the stick and threw it into the shallow eddy swirling along the bank.

At first, Ward's emotions were too muddled to separate. Relief, annoyance, amusement and bewilderment all vied for expression, but thankfulness won out. She was safe. He felt foolish for jumping to conclusions.

Pokey greeted him with wet paws and a wagging tail spraying droplets of cold water. As Ward dropped on the ground beside Shannon, she looked at him in surprise. "How did you find me?"

"My great grandfather was a scout."

"Really?"

"Yes, really." His smile faded. "But you shouldn't take off by yourself like that. It's easy to get disoriented and end up miles from where you think you are."

"I'm not as inept as you think I am," she retorted. "Believe it or not, I didn't have any trouble finding my way to the stream. And you didn't have to come looking for me. I'm sure you have more pressing things to do."

Ouch. Her tone was as sharp as a cactus barb. "Do you want to tell me what's the matter, or shall we play twenty questions?"

She ignored his teasing grin. "It shouldn't take twenty. One ought to do. What in blazes am I doing back here?"

He ignored her accusing tone. "You're here because you made that choice," he answered evenly.

"I'm not sure I did," she argued. "I think it just happened."

"Nobody lives a choiceless life, Shannon. Sometimes we make a decision not to make a choice, and that in itself is a choice. Sometimes we let others make choices for us, but that's not you, Shannon. You're here because that's what you decided to do."

"Well, it was a mistake...a terrible mistake." She glared at him as if she dared him to deny it.

Obviously, she wanted him to argue that she'd made the right choice or admit that he was responsible for it. He wasn't going to go there. The truth was that he'd been totally surprised by her sudden decision. At the time, he had truly believed there had been some kind of divine intervention in answer to his prayers for her well being, but he knew if he offered such a possibility, she would scoff at him. They couldn't even talk about the situation in terms of where the good Lord might be leading them.

"Why do you think it was a mistake?" he asked, searching her eyes for some glimpse of insight that he needed to understand where she was coming from.

"It's obvious, isn't it? I've put my life on hold—and for what?"

"To be of help?"

"Who needs me? Not anyone, that's pretty obvious. It took me about fifteen minutes back here to figure that out. Not Tara. She has you and Beth to love and care for her. And you have a family and a ranch to run and dreams to realize. There's nothing I can add by being here. Nothing. It's a waste of my time.''

"Are you sure? What about this moment? Drawing in the freshness of pine-scented air. Listening to the soothing water. How many hours in a crowded office are worth this peace and quiet?''

"More than I can afford.''

"Are you sure? Why not take this opportunity to let yourself enjoy a different pace and—''

"Don't you understand? I have to be doing something about my finances, my future, instead of pretending that all is well when it isn't.''

He reached for her hand, but she stood up, ignoring the gesture. "Do you want to see if I can find my way back?''

"I'd rather sit here for a few minutes and figure this thing out.''

"There's nothing to figure out. I made a mistake, and it only took me an hour to find it out.''

She started through the trees, not even looking to see if he and Pokey were coming. What in the world had set her off like that, Ward wondered as he followed her. He could have overtaken her, but he decided to treat her like a stubborn horse, let her have her head and see where she ended up. If she started moving too far in the wrong direction, he'd stop her before she got into trouble.

Shannon turned her head once to see if he and the pup were following, then she increased her pace. Much to his surprise, she slipped through the grove of trees and brush without difficulty and came out of the wooded area almost where the shortest way to the ranch house began.

At the edge of the meadow, she stopped. What's the matter with you? she asked herself. She was suddenly ashamed of her childish tantrum. Taking out her mistake on him wasn't fair. He hadn't put any pressure on her. The decision had been hers. It wasn't his fault she had given in to some irrational impulse. He didn't deserve to have any added responsibilities, and she had seen a concerned tightness in his expression when he sat down beside her.

"I'm sorry if I caused you any worry," she said when he caught up with her. "I just thought a walk might clear my head, and Pokey needed a run."

"It's all right. Just tell someone next time where you're going. I know you're used to being independent, but in this part of the country, we depend upon each other. None of us can do our own thing without it affecting everyone else."

"I'm not used to thinking in those terms. I'm used to going my own way."

He turned her around to face him. "I want to take care of you, Shannon. Not because it's a responsibility. Not because it's a duty. I just want to take care of you."

"I don't need—"

"I know." He sighed. "You don't need anyone."

Just you, she admitted silently.

He searched her expression, and as he tightened his arms around her, she let herself be drawn into the warmth of his embrace. She waited for him to speak of the building attraction between them. If he would compromise and set aside the issue of her spiritual beliefs or lack of them, maybe, they could find a solution to their other differences. Even as she longed for him to speak some words of love to her, he slowly set her away from him.

"We'd better get back to the house before they send out someone to look for us," he said gently.

She managed to cover her disappointment with a bright smile and a nod. Once again, she'd let her guard down, desperately wanting him to declare himself, but he had sidestepped any commitment. Was she completely misreading his attentions to her? She had the feeling he was waiting for some miraculous conversion that would change her into the kind of woman he wanted in his life. She was hurt, disappointed and angry, but she wasn't about to pretend to be something she wasn't for any man. What you see is what you get, Ward Dawson.

When they came into the kitchen, Beth was talking earnestly to Ted. "Well, now, that's a worry, isn't it?"

"What's a worry?" Ward asked.

"The wildfire," Ted answered, a deep frown on his young face. "It's moving toward Box Canyon. If they don't get it stopped before it starts down that draw, it'll hit my grandma's place, for sure."

"Maybe it's time you moved Rachel out of there. You don't want to wait until the last minute," Ward warned.

"That's what we were talking about," Beth said. "What are you going to do with a stubborn woman like Rachel, hog-tie her and carry her bodily out of her home?''

"If necessary," Ward answered firmly.

"She's agreed to start packing some things, just in case," Ted said. "The problem is, she's moving kinda slow these days." He hesitated and then added, "I was wondering if one of the women could go and help her."

Ward frowned. "I don't know. Beth's got her hands full, and the other women have children—"

"I could go."

There was a pointed silence while everyone looked at Shannon as if they'd forgotten she was even there. The skepticism on their faces sparked her indignation.

"I'm perfectly capable of helping Ted's grandmother pack up some of her things," she insisted.

"Sure you are," Beth said, nodding her head in approval. "It's kind of you to offer."

"Her place is pretty isolated," Ted warned.

That's not the half of it, Ward thought. Ted's grandmother lived in a tiny three-room log house that had been on the homestead property for years. No electricity. No heating. Only well water for the kitchen and other uses. No modern conveniences. No neighbors for miles.

"Gram's place is pretty rustic," Ted said, as if his thoughts were running along the same line.

"You might call it ramshackle," Ward offered bluntly. All the surrounding land had been leased out for grazing, providing Rachel with her only income except what Ted's wages added. By the wildest stretch of his imagination, Ward could not picture Shannon spending even a couple of hours in such primitive surroundings. She could get hurt and create more problems for Rachel without realizing it.

"No, Shannon. It's out of the question," he said flatly.

"I beg your pardon." Her temper flared, and her eyes shot fire at him. "If Ted needs someone to help his grandmother, and I volunteered, I fail to see why you even need to offer your opinion on the matter." She used the same brisk tone and unyielding eye contact that she employed when challenged by some belligerent adversary in a board meeting.

The only sound in the kitchen was a teakettle making a merry whistle on the stove. Both Ted and Beth lowered their eyes and didn't say anything.

"All right, Shannon," Ward said with reluctance, knowing that anything he said she would brush aside as interference. "I withdraw my objections. I know that Rachel will be happy to see you." *Forgive me, Lord, for the lie.* Ward knew the crusty old lady would delight in putting a city girl through a briar patch of demands and embarrassments.

Shannon ignored Ward's warning frown as she turned to Ted. "When do we leave, Ted?"

"We could go right now. It's about an hour's drive. I'll drop you off and then head back for the evening chores." He looked at Ward for approval. "Okay, boss?"

"Fine," he said, even though he wanted to suggest that Shannon wait until morning. That way he could drive her to Rachel's and bring her back when she had a look at the place and met Ted's grandmother, but

Shannon's hands-off attitude toward him rang loud and clear.

"I'll fix up a basket to send with you," Beth said. "I don't think Rachel cooks much anymore."

"I'll pack up my few things and be ready to go when you are, Ted," Shannon said, but her stubborn bravado was for nothing.

The telephone rang, and Ward answered it. "Yes, he's here." He handed the receiver to Ted.

He listened, then quickly answered, "Yes, sir. I understand. Thanks for the warning. Yes, I'll tell Ward." He hung up and said anxiously, "I've got to get Grams out of there tonight. The fire's broken over the ridge and is heading down Box Canyon."

"I'll go with you."

"No, you're to call Chief McGrady right away," Ted told him. "Something about a helicopter going down on Silver Mountain." Ted hesitated. "Can I borrow your truck? I'll need it to bring down Gram's stuff. I'll leave my Jeep."

"Sure. Good enough," Ward agreed. They exchanged keys.

"Tell Rachel that she can stay with us. We've got plenty of room," Beth lied.

Ted nodded. "I'm out of here."

Beth shook her head as he disappeared out the back door. "I'll wager he'll have to carry Rachel out kicking and screaming. She won't leave willingly even if the roof's falling in on her."

Shannon felt completely at a loss to keep up with what was happening. Once again she felt like excess baggage, and her stomach tightened as Ward made his call. From his side of the conversation, she knew that one of the aircraft dropping water had gone down and that air reconnaissance had failed to spot the wreckage. They had called on Ward because he knew the area and had experience with a rescue unit.

"Well, if the copter went down in that thick timber on this side of the mountain, it'll take a ground search to find it," Ward said, frowning. "Yes, sir, I probably know that old mountain as well as anyone. There's an old Jeep trail up to those old mine diggings." He listened for a long moment. "Yes, sir, as soon as it's daylight, I'll head up that way and radio you if I see anything." He thoughtfully hung up the phone, then turned to the two women staring at him. "Well, I guess it's a good thing Ted left me his Jeep. I'm going to take a little ride up Silver Mountain in the morning."

"Too bad Ted isn't here to go with you," Beth said, shaking her head. "Why does everything happen at once?"

"I'll go with you."

"What?" Ward looked at Shannon with an expression he might have used for one of Tara's foolish pronouncements.

"I said that I'll go with you. My offer to help Rachel has gone down the tube, so I'm available."

"I really don't think that's a good idea—"

"You can't use a second pair of eyes?"

"It isn't that," he answered quickly, both amused and irritated by her insistence. "I haven't taken that Jeep road for a couple of years. I don't know what condition it's in, and I may have to leave the Jeep and do some demanding hiking."

"So—"

He stared at her as if he couldn't believe he was having this conversation. "For starters, there's the matter of hiking shoes, and some serviceable clothing for this kind of outing."

Beth cleared her throat. "I believe Kenny's mom wears the same size shoe. Shannon, wasn't Alice trying on one of your summer sandals? I'll bet she'd willingly make a temporary loan of her hiking boots and maybe a heavy jacket. Your blue jeans ought to do fine with a couple of sweaters. Don't you think so, Ward?"

Ward stared at his sister. There was no doubt about whose side she was suddenly on.

"This could turn out to be a very demanding search," he argued.

"Then I would think you could use an extra body along," Beth answered flatly. "You were going to let Shannon go off by herself. Wouldn't you'd rather have her along with you?" She eyed him frankly. "Maybe the two of you ought to share a few experiences together."

Shannon sent her a grateful look. "Let's take a vote," she suggested factiously.

Ward was smart enough to know the odds were stacked against him. He decided it was no use wasting his breath, trying to argue with a couple of hardheaded women.

He still had reservations about taking Shannon along, but suddenly the idea of being with her began to outweigh his reluctance.

"All right, but you may end up sitting in the Jeep," he warned. "There's not even daylight left to start up that mountain now. We'll head out as soon as it's dawn.''

"Yes, sir.'' She gave him a mock salute, and she could hear Beth chuckling as she hurried upstairs to get ready.

She collected what she needed from Alice Gordon, then peeked in Tara's room. She wanted to tell her that she wouldn't be seeing her the next day, but the little girl was sound asleep. She was obviously tired from the excitement of coming home.

Tara looked so small and fragile that Shannon wanted to take her in her arms and just hold her. A strange kind of ache suddenly made Shannon realize that somehow the little girl had slipped through the protective guard she had placed around herself. She turned away quickly, knowing in her heart that it was too late to deny the deep need to belong to someone— even to a child and a dedicated man who found her wanting.

Chapter Twelve

Ward and Shannon left the ranch the next morning just as the night sky was giving way to a gunmetal gray. The condition of the Jeep road would determine how quickly they could reach the old mining ruins near the crest of the mountain. Ward hoped they would sight the downed plane before nightfall or assure themselves it had not gone down on the southern slope of Silver Mountain.

He glanced at Shannon, sitting beside him, and couldn't tell if the early morning rising was responsible for her silent behavior or if she was having second thoughts about insisting she go with him. He was certainly having second thoughts. In the cold light of morning, the decision seemed ridiculous. What was he thinking? He had no idea what the day would bring. He'd been swept along by her forceful insistence that she help Ted's grandmother, and when that didn't work out, she'd turned that into a determination to go with him. His sister's remarks hadn't helped at all.

"We should reach the base of the mountain just about the time the sun comes up," he said over the roar of the engine. "Beth packed a thermos and some egg sandwiches for breakfast."

"Sounds delicious."

He silently chuckled. She lied beautifully. That strong independent stubborn streak of hers would never let her admit she'd made one heck of a mistake by insisting that she come along. He bet there'd be no whining from her. She was wearing an unbecoming too-large jacket, a flannel plaid shirt, jeans and borrowed hiking boots. And yet she had never looked more feminine or appealing. It was as if she belonged beside him in an old Jeep, bumping over a rough road at the breaking of a new day. An emotion he was startled to recognize as pure contentment surged through him.

"Why are you smiling?" she asked in a slightly defensive tone. She was aware of his clear brown eyes appraising her even though the brim of his tan cowboy hat put his face in shadow. "Don't you think I look like the well-dressed woman ready for a rescue mission?"

"Absolutely."

"I can do this, Ward. You have to give me a chance. I know I haven't exactly demonstrated that I'm the strong, outdoor type, but all my life, I've been able to learn what I need to know and made a success of it. I want to be a help, not a tagalong. Do you understand?"

He nodded. He understood, all right, but the truth was that she didn't have a glimmer of an idea what was involved. Once the Jeep road ran out without any

sign of the wreckage, a climb would have to be made
to reach the rocky promontory giving an overview of
the southern slope of the mountain. She'd never be able
to keep up with him. He was used to the high altitude
and oxygen-thin air, but she would need repeated rest
stops to make it. He had already decided she would
stay with the Jeep.

"What are you thinking?" she demanded, her eyes
fixed on his face.

"About having a cup of that coffee," he lied. "How
about pouring me one? We'd better have breakfast before we reach the base of the mountain." He knew
she'd need something in her stomach before they
started the harrowing climb. He just prayed that sections of the road hadn't been washed out since he'd
last driven it. "I think Beth put in some cinnamon rolls,
too. And who knows what else? That sister of mine
knows how to fill a food hamper."

"She's a wonderful cook," Shannon said, with a
hint of envy in her tone.

As they ate breakfast in the jolting Jeep, the rising
sun spread a tapestry of orange, pink and red across
the eastern horizon.

"Wow. Isn't God magnificent?" Ward breathed rev-
erently, gazing at it. "He gives us a masterpiece like
that every morning and evening. Just looking at it cre-
ates a sense of the divine, doesn't it?"

She responded honestly. "I've never looked at a sun-
rise in that way."

"It's simple. When you start looking for God's miracles, they're all over the place." He chuckled. "Tara
and I made a list of God's miracles one day, starting

with the seeds for Beth's garden. At first, Tara wouldn't believe that each tiny seed knew the exact kind and number of leaves to grow and what color each flower should be, but as Beth's garden grew, she witnessed the miracle.'' He glanced at Shannon. ''It's the same with people, you know. We're all programmed for a miracle.''

''Oh, really?'' she answered with obvious disbelief.

''Yep. There's a divine plan for our lives. Ready and waiting when we're born.''

''Are you talking about fate?''

''Nope, I'm talking about the choice we have to follow our own desires or give ourselves up to the plan God has for each of us.'' He waited to see what her response was going to be. If only she would lower her defenses, he thought hopefully, and trust that God was not going to disappoint her the way other people in her life had. He knew she was afraid to take that step and he didn't know how to convince her to make it.

She stared out the window for a long moment without answering. Then she leaned her head back against the seat rest and closed her eyes. ''It's too early in the morning for a theological debate.''

He sighed, knowing that the religious gulf between them was still as wide as ever.

When they reached the base of Silver Mountain, Ward tightened his grip on the steering wheel. ''Well, here we go.''

Shannon sat up straight. This was a road? Surely, Ward had made a mistake. He didn't intend to drive up the side of the mountain on this narrow crumbling shelf, did he? One glance at the way he'd set his strong chin told her he intended to do exactly that. When he had mentioned a Jeep trail, she had thought he was using a western euphemism for a scenic western drive.

As they began to climb, she could hear loose rocks spitting out from under the wheels and feel the Jeep sliding in the loose earth. Her mouth went dry. She'd already had one experience going over the side of a mountain road. She might not be as lucky this time.

"How far?" she managed to ask, trying to keep from looking out the window as the ground fell away below them.

"The trail is about ten miles," Ward answered evenly, silently adding, If it hasn't washed out or fallen away. The road had certainly deteriorated a lot since he'd driven it. Once this Jeep trail had been listed in a Colorado guide to old mining camps, but it was obvious that was no longer the case. He doubted if there was much left on the mountain except mine tailings and gaping tunnel holes left by disappointed prospectors.

Leaning forward over the wheel, he searched for ways to avoid dangerous rocks and washouts in the narrow trail. The engine was straining in the higher elevation, and Ward wished Ted had kept the Jeep in better condition. What if one of the old tires blew? What if— He cut off that train of thought and in his mind substituted a favorite scripture.

He will give His angels charge over thee to keep thee in all thy ways. They shall bear thee up in their hands, lest they dash thy foot against a stone.

"Amen," he murmured.

Shannon shot a quick glance at him. Things must really be bad if Ward was praying. Her stomach took a sickening plunge. She swallowed to get some moisture in her dry mouth.

The rough trail twisted back on itself like a thin serpent.

Sometimes it looked as if a part of it had fallen away and was too narrow for the Jeep's wheels. In these places, Ward braked, eyed the passage ahead, then eased the Jeep forward, almost scraping the side of the mountain on his side. When they came to a passage wide enough to get his door open, he got out and surveyed the wooded areas above and below.

"See anything?" Shannon asked hopefully, and every time, he shook his head as he got back in.

"It's likely the helicopter went down at a much higher elevation than this. We don't even know if it's on this side of the mountain. Chief McGrady has another scout combing the north side, and they'll radio me if they find anything." He smiled at Shannon. "I bet you'd be real disappointed to cut our Jeep ride short."

"Try me," she answered dryly.

"Believe it or not, some people pay good money for a trip like this."

"Some people have a suicide complex, too, but I'm not one of them," she assured him, trying to return his smile. The fact that she had insisted on coming was not lost on either of them. She silently vowed she'd do her best not to let him see how terrified she was. "If you say this is fun, I'll try to believe it."

Despite her attempt at levity, he could see her hands

clenched so tightly her fingernails were biting into her soft flesh. Impulsively, he stopped the Jeep and pulled her close.

"It's going to be all right. I'm going to take good care of you," he whispered as his lips touched her soft cheek. "I'm glad you're here," he murmured with an honesty that didn't make any sense at all.

"Me, too," she said honestly. Even as they were precariously perched on the side of a mountain cliff, she was glad she was there with him.

He lightly kissed the tip of her nose, pulled away and started driving again. Looking back, they could see the dark haze rising on the far horizon where the wildfires were raging. Ward thought about Ted and his grandmother and silently prayed they would get safely out of the canyon. He glanced at Shannon, thankful she was here beside him instead of at Rachel's place. "We're almost there," he assured her as they took the last switchback.

"So soon?" Shannon quipped. Each hour had seemed like ten. She couldn't bear to think about the paralyzing return trip.

"This is it," he said as the road ended abruptly in an open area. "End of the line."

Gaping black holes and mounds of tailings dotted the nearby slopes. Weathered piles of wood hinted at a bygone prospecting frenzy.

As they got out of the Jeep, he said, "We'll hike a short distance in both directions. Chief McGrady said that last communication they had from the missing helicopter could have been in this area. If we don't see anything at this elevation, I'll take a look from that crest up there.'' He pointed to a rocky bluff high above the place where they stood.

Shannon was aware he had used the pronoun *I*, but she didn't argue. At the moment, she was too grateful to have solid earth under her feet. She followed him as he led the way along a rocky shelf that gave a good view of the wooded slopes below. He had given her a small pair of binoculars that belonged to Beth.

''Look for any sign of damaged treetops, a glint of metal, anything that stands out as unusual and unnatural,'' he instructed.

They pushed through scratchy thickets and climbed on top of large boulders to get a better view. She was grateful for borrowed hiking boots and the long-sleeved flannel shirt. After searching the landscape in every direction in vain, they returned to the Jeep.

''Let's grab a bite of lunch,'' Ward said, peering at the sky. He didn't like the way darkening clouds were gathering on the western horizon. Everyone had been praying for rain, but it would certainly play havoc with their ground search if it arrived in the next few hours.

''Why are you frowning?'' Shannon asked as she swallowed a bite of egg sandwich, which to her surprise tasted wonderful.

''Was I?'' he asked in mock innocence. He brushed a crumb from his mouth. Took a swallow of water from his canteen, then stood up. ''While you settle comfy in the Jeep for a spell, I reckon I'll take a little stroll.''

She wasn't fooled by his good ol' boy jargon. He was telling her to stay put while he continued the search. ''And if you see something?''

''I'll radio McGrady, come back to the Jeep, and

we'll wait for a rescue team. They'll have medics and personnel to handle any victims. I should be able to make it to the rim in a couple of hours, have a look and be back before dusk.'' He strapped on his backpack, made sure the radio was fastened to his belt, then bent and kissed her lightly. "Stay put."

She nodded, clinging to his hand an extra second. "You be careful," she ordered.

"Yes, ma'am." He gave her that winning grin of his, turned away and in a long, purposeful stride headed up the ravine that cut into the mountain as it rose toward the crest of the mountain.

Shannon fully intended to do as he ordered, but as soon as Ward disappeared from view, her imagination fired all kinds of images of him in trouble. Slipping. Falling. Getting hurt with no one around to see it.

Her thoughts whirled. If she hadn't insisted on coming, he could have brought one of his ranch hands, and Shannon knew Ward wouldn't have ordered him to stay behind. Guilt stabbed at her. He'd given in to her stubborn determination to come at the cost of his safety.

Grabbing her borrowed jacket, she took off after him. She was confident she could overtake him without any trouble because he'd only had a few minutes' head start. She soon discovered she had miscalculated two things—the swiftness of his long stride and the demands of the increased altitude on her breathing and energy.

Every time she stopped to catch her breath, she knew he was getting farther and farther ahead. As the stands of trees and undergrowth became thicker, a quiver of panic set in. He could have veered off in any direction. She saw nothing but thick stands of trees, tumbled rocks and decaying logs. As she turned to look in every direction, she suddenly wasn't sure which way she'd come.

I can't be lost.

"Ward. Ward? Where are you?"

Her voice bounced right back at her. She strained to hear something besides the loud thumping of her heart. Nothing.

She called his name again.

Suddenly he was there, standing at the top of a mound of boulders just beyond the place where she had stopped.

"There you are," she gasped.

A flood of relief surged through her body. But when she saw his expression, she wished with all her heart she could disappear. She had never seen him angry. His usually soft brown eyes were hard as steel, and his mouth was rigid with controlled fury. Instantly, her rationale for disobeying his orders seemed terribly shallow and without merit. She swallowed hard and braced herself for his fury.

"What part of stay in the Jeep didn't you understand, Shannon?" he asked coldly.

"None of it," she answered with her usual stubbornness. She forced herself to meet his angry gaze squarely. She'd been on the hot seat plenty of times in her job and had decided that leading with her chin was the only way to handle a foul-up—especially one of her own making. "I was worried about you. You said the other searchers are on the far side of the mountain.'' She hoped the nervous tremor in the pit of her stomach didn't show. ''So I decided to come along— whether you like it or not.''

At first she thought he was going to turn and leave her standing there, breathless, frightened and ashamed of herself. ''I don't have time to take you back,'' he said shortly. She was relieved when she saw the stiffness around his mouth ease slightly. ''I guess you win—for now.''

''I'll keep up, I promise.''

He nodded, held out his hand and helped her over the mound of boulders. With grim determination, she did her best not to lag too far behind as he led the way up the rugged slope. They skirted narrow ledges, crawled on all fours and fought through thick drifts of trees and bushes.

Because going straight up was impossible in the craggy terrain, they hiked in zigzag patterns around rock ledges, steep inclines and cliffs. There were still mounds of tailings and mining tunnels, and Shannon marveled at the tenacity of men searching for a fortune on this craggy hillside.

What a waste, she thought. What people wouldn't do for money. Quickly she shoved away the truth that she was the one who had been struggling all her adult life to find success in a world where money was the driving force.

''You okay?'' Ward asked as he looked back to check on her.

She nodded, hoping he wouldn't notice that she was limping slightly. Her borrowed hiking boots had begun to rub a blister on her right heel.

They stopped repeatedly to survey their surroundings in every direction. The hope was always there that they would spot the wreckage and could radio the location to a rescue team searching the other side, but each time they were disappointed.

It became clear to Ward that Shannon was drawing on every bit of endurance she could summon. He wished there was some way to make things easier for her. Even though she'd asked for the grueling climb, he knew misguided concern over his welfare was responsible for her stubborn determination to come with him. Unfortunately her good intentions could very well be an additional burden he could ill afford. She had slowed him down, and time was of the essence.

The wind had quickened, and he kept looking at the darkening sky. He knew how quickly a summer storm could form in these mountains, and climbing would be more perilous than ever when the ground was wet and slippery. *Lord, I don't know how this is going to turn out, but I trust that You do.*

"What do you think?" Shannon asked, searching his face.

"It could blow over," he said. "Sometimes we don't get more than a sprinkle from clouds like that." He prayed that this was one of those times.

When they reached a small waterfall trickling down from the rocks above, both of them were ready for a break. Shannon's chest was burning more than she was willing to admit. She eased down on a patch of green near the pool of water and resisted the urge to take off her boot.

Ward quickly filled his canteen and handed it to

Shannon. He was about to sit down beside her when he heard something.

"What was that sound?"

Shannon looked at him, puzzled. "The water falling?"

He shook his head. Not water. More of a thrashing noise. He swung his eyes in the direction of a nearby grove of trees.

"What's the matter?" Shannon asked, watching his face as his eyes narrowed.

"I'm not sure," he answered. The pool could be a watering hole for wild animals. There were plenty of black bears and wildcats in these mountain forests. Several times he'd seen mountain goats scampering over rocky cliffs at lower elevations. It could be that they were coming this way for water.

"I don't hear anything." She strained to listen, but couldn't hear anything besides the gurgling, tumbling water.

He waved his hand. "Get behind those rocks and stay out of sight."

She started to argue, but for once in her life, she did as she was told—well, almost. She didn't stay out of sight. She couldn't keep from peering around the large boulders. What was out there? She couldn't even begin to imagine what kind of danger might be just a few feet away.

Ward moved slowly forward, holding his head in a listening position. He still couldn't identify the sound, but no animal he knew about made that much noise. Very slowly, Ward walked away from the waterfall toward the heavy stand of trees.

Shannon wanted to scream at him to come back. He didn't carry a gun. What if some wild creature attacked him? She lurched to her feet. Stay out of sight. His order vibrated in her ears, and only the thought of his anger kept her from bolting after him.

Ward made his way into a dense stand of evergreens. Now that he was away from the rushing water, the thrashing sound grew louder.

What was it?

He could hear the snap of broken twigs and the crunch of ground cover. He pressed up behind a large tree. Something was coming right toward him.

What was it?

His breath caught as the heavy undergrowth parted, and he saw what was making the noise.

"Dear God," Ward breathed as a man dressed in a blood-splattered pilot's uniform staggered into view and nearly fell at his feet.

Chapter Thirteen

Ward bolted forward and caught the man before his knees gave out. "I've got you. Take it easy."

He was a small man with graying dark hair.

His face was scratched and bruised. One eye was nearly swollen shut. His uniform was torn and covered with stickers from wild mountain shrubs. "I—I— we—" he stammered.

"We've been looking for you." Ward raised his voice and called, "Shannon."

When she heard him calling her name, she lurched to her feet. What was wrong? What had happened to him? Not hesitating for even a split second, she ran toward his voice. The horror of his struggling in the savage grip of a wild beast was in her mind's eye as she bolted through the trees.

When she saw him half carrying a blood-covered man, she had trouble registering the truth. She gasped in disbelief. "Is it…"

"One of the flyers. Get the first aid kit out of my pack." He eased the man down on a green patch near the waterfall. "You're okay now."

"Pete," he croaked.

"That's your name?" Ward asked kneeling beside him.

"No... Pete is still in the plane." He gasped for breath. "Hurt. Needs help," he mumbled in a hoarse, exhausted voice.

"All right, we'll get him help. Here, take a drink. Not too much."

Ward put the canteen to the man's trembling lips, and a flood of questions instantly swarmed in his head. How far had the man walked? He needed information to relay to McGrady as soon as possible. Where had the helicopter gone down? Ward forced himself to wait for answers.

Shannon opened the small first aid kit and eased down beside the injured man. There were several cuts on the pilot's face, crusted with blood, but none of them seemed to be still bleeding. Shannon knew nothing about nursing, but there were no signs of broken bones. Several times she'd passed up the chance to take first aid classes that the Red Cross offered. She had asked herself, When will I ever need those? Never in a dozen lifetimes would she have imagined that the answer to that question was a situation like this.

A warning rumble of thunder jerked their eyes upward. Ward groaned as fast-moving dark thunderhead clouds blanketed nearby craggy peaks.

"We've got to find shelter."

"Where?" Did Ward know of a mountain cabin some place close?

"Help me get him to his feet," he ordered, ignoring her question. He motioned her to take one side while he took the other. He knew these mountain storms. In a matter of minutes they could be caught in a blinding downpour. With the exhausted man stumbling between them, they headed down the slope they had climbed a few minutes earlier.

Shannon choked back a protest. Why were they retracing their steps? What was he thinking? They couldn't possibly make it to the Jeep before the storm hit.

When Ward veered off in an unfamiliar area, she became completely disoriented. In the darkening forest, she couldn't see what direction they were heading.

Where was Ward taking them?

Vibrating thunder sounded like heavenly artillery drawn across the skies. Almost immediately the gentle spray of cool drops thickened. Ward urged them forward, moving as fast as the exhausted man stumbling between them would allow.

"We're almost there," he shouted over the pounding rain.

Almost where? Shannon squinted ahead. Then she knew.

Through the thickening rain, she could see a gaping black hole in the side of the mountain. They were headed for an abandoned mine tunnel.

Oh, no! A surge of panic whipped through her. She couldn't do it. She'd never been able to stand confining, dark spaces. Cowering in a dank, dark mine was as terrifying as the thought of being buried alive. She would rather stay out in the drowning rain. When they were just a few feet away from the mine's entrance, the exhausted man's legs gave out.

"I've got you," Ward said, lifting him on his shoulders, carrying him the rest of the way.

Shannon watched as they disappeared into the depths of the black tunnel. As sliding mud and gushing water poured down, she couldn't make herself follow Ward into that dark abyss. Visions of earth tumbling down on her kept her rooted in the driving rain. She closed her eyes against the spears of lightning and the cannonlike booms of thunder.

"Shannon," Ward barked as he dashed into the rain.

"No, I can't—"

He ignored her sobbing. With one swift movement, he lifted her in his arms and carried her into the black hole.

He set her on the ground, and she bit her lip, struggling to hold back a rising hysteria. "I...I can't stay here."

"Yes, you can," he said firmly as if he were talking to his five-year-old daughter instead of a twenty-eight-year-old adult. He lifted her chin so she had to look directly into his eyes. "It's safe."

Safe? The word was a mockery. Echoing thunder vibrated from the walls, and the dark passage looked ready to let tons of dirt slide down upon them at any moment. It must have been years since anyone had been inside the dark, crumbling mine tunnel. It was filled with tumbled rocks and rotted wood, and it had a penetrating dank smell. Even in the dim light, she could see where the earth and timber had fallen away from the dirt walls.

"We can't stay here," she protested vehemently.

"We have to," he answered firmly. "And I need your help. That's why you tagged along, remember?"

But I didn't bargain for this, she raged silently, swallowing hard against a rising quivering in her stomach. She hated the way he was reminding her it was her fault she was here—even if it was true.

"You're not going to faint on me, are you?" he asked anxiously as she wavered.

"No, I'm not going to faint," she answered as firmly as she could, silently hoping it was true.

"Good," Ward said. He knew how hard she'd tried to measure up to the demands she had invited by coming with him. And he understood and sympathized with her feelings about the mine.

The first time his father had taken him into one, he'd wanted to run shrieking out of the horrid place. He couldn't breathe. The darkness seemed to claw at him. His eyes were blinded by the lack of light. Those feelings had never quite gone away, and if it hadn't been for the injured man, he would have taken his chances in the forest, lightning or no lightning.

"It's going to be all right, Shannon," he said gently as he brushed a damp strand of hair from her face. "Trust me. Okay?"

"Okay," she echoed, drawing on his warm breath touching her cheek and the gentle stroke of his hand. This was no time to exert her stubborn independence.

"Right now, we need to keep this fellow warm."

"How do we do that?" she asked, struggling to focus on something besides the echoing sounds of their voices and the dripping of water seeping down the dirt walls.

"I've got a poncho in my backpack. Let's get it on him right away. I'll try to make radio contact with McGrady as soon as the electrical interference from the storm will let me. Right now, I need to get all the information I can about where the helicopter went down."

As he bent over the man, Ward was relieved to see his eyes still open and tracking. His breathing was rapid, but Ward thought he looked fairly alert for someone who was soaking wet and exhausted.

"We're waiting out the storm here," Ward told him.

He gave a faint nod to show he understood.

"I'm Ward Dawson. I'm one of the people sent out to look for you. From your last transmission, they thought you might have made it to this side of the mountain. What's your name?"

"Ross Johnson," he whispered with blue lips.

"Okay, Ross, we're going to try and get you warm," Ward said, and covered him with his heavy poncho. He never went out riding without it, and more than once he'd been grateful for its warmth.

"Do you feel like talking a little, Ross?" Ward asked, knowing the man might pass out on him any time. If the storm hadn't come up, he would have quizzed the man as soon as he'd found him. There was a rising urgency to get as much information as quickly as possible about the location of the downed craft so he could get that information to McGrady right away. "Just take your time."

With halting, labored breaths, Ross told what had happened. The helicopter had developed mechanical problems. Ross had tried to set it down on the high bluff, but it had slid off into a deep ravine.

"I blacked out…stayed there all night. Pete was hurt bad, but he was still breathing." His cold lips quivered. "When it got light, I crawled out of the wreckage."

"Where was the sun?"

"In front of me…east."

Slowly, Ward was able to get answers to some pointed questions that gave him a good idea of the general location of the downed craft. From Ross's description of the terrain, Ward was pretty sure the aircraft had slid into the deep draw in the mountain just west of the waterfall. Ross couldn't have hiked very far in his condition.

"I was trying to climb where I might be seen if a rescue copter came over. But I had to keep stopping…not enough strength."

"You did great," Ward assured him. He knew that, despite Ross's valiant effort, making it up the steep incline to any place he might be seen would have been unlikely in his condition.

The pilot must have realized it, too. "It was pure luck that you found me."

"It wasn't luck," Ward corrected gently. "It was divine guidance." *Thank you, Lord.*

The man closed his eyes without answering.

Shannon's heart missed a beat. "Is he—"

Ward felt for a pulse. "His heartbeat is steady. I think he's just fallen into an exhausted sleep. He's pushed himself too hard. We've got to keep him dry and warm."

"How are we going to do that?"

Shannon hugged herself against a rising wave of shivers. Her hair lay plastered against her head. Although her borrowed jacket and her jeans had shed some of the rain, they were still damp. Fortunately the plaid shirt was still dry, and the heavy boots had kept her feet warm.

Ward glanced out the mine opening. No sign that the storm was passing over. In fact, if anything, the wind had shifted and was stronger than before. If the storm clouds got hung up on these mountains, the rain could settle in for hours. A downpour like this one would put out the wildfire, and the scorched hillsides would give off smoldering whiffs of smoke. He could imagine the jubilation of the evacuated families. The crisis would be over in a matter of hours if the sky kept dumping sheets of rain in the area.

"A good storm for ending the wildfires," he said, knowing it was the worst kind of weather for a rescue. His immediate concern was bringing two injured pilots to safety. "We just have to wait and see if the storm clouds are going to lift. In the meantime, we need to handle things as best we can."

She nodded, but at the moment, she didn't see a glimmer of best in the situation. He rose to his feet, reached into his backpack and took out a small flashlight.

"Where are you going?" A sudden panic shot

through her as she realized he was going to walk into the tunnel.

"I'll be back in a minute. You stay here."

As he disappeared into the engulfing darkness, she couldn't have forced herself to follow him. Where had he gone? She needed his presence to ease her raw-edged nerves. Why had he left so abruptly? Was he aware of a new danger? Her sense of claustrophobia mingled with a new rising fear.

When she saw the bobbing flashlight coming toward her in the dark tunnel, she jerked to her feet. As his shadowy figure came into view, she saw that he was carrying something.

"What is it?" she asked, unable to make out what he was clutching in his arms.

"Dry timber."

"Timber?" she echoed.

"We need to make a fire as soon as the rain stops." He walked to the mouth of the tunnel and dropped the splintered dry wood in a pile just short of the entrance.

"Do we have to wait until then?" she protested, hugging herself against a wave of shivers.

"Yep, I'm afraid so. A fire burns up oxygen, so we can't build one in an enclosed passage," he explained. "In any case the smoke would drive us out...so we'll wait." He eased down on the ground beside her, and put an arm around her shoulders. "At least there's plenty of dry timber lying around for fuel."

Shannon failed to find comfort in the reassurance. It was all she could do to keep her teeth from chattering.

"Once I got caught out in a storm like this," Ward told her. "I was so cold I thought my blood was turning into red icicles, but I kept thinking about how warm I was going to be when the sun came out and the shivers went away. Strange, isn't it, how our mind can control our body?''

"Are you telling me that if I think I'm sitting here getting a sunburn, my body will believe it?''

He chuckled. "Well, I couldn't guarantee it, but keep that thought, and see what happens.''

She gratefully pressed her chilled face against his chest. The strong rhythm of his breathing settled the wild flutter of her heart and the warmth of his strong, muscular body seemed miraculously to seep into hers. She'd never felt this kind of close bonding with anyone. In fact, she'd never been comfortable being too physically close to anyone. She'd always insisted on her own space and made sure no one violated it by getting too close. She stiffened when someone tried to hug her, but being in Ward's arms was different. She welcomed his physical closeness with a bliss she wouldn't have thought possible.

"Better?'' Ward asked as the shivering of her body began to ease.

"Yes. Much better.''

He rested his head against Shannon's, dismayed by the depths of the feelings he had for her. Many times in his life he had been confused and uncertain, but never as much as from the moment he'd met her. Nothing about their relationship made sense. He'd been determined not to make a mistake when he married again, and Shannon Hensley was nothing like the mate he thought he was looking for. The kind of life she led was completely foreign to him. Her ambitions had led her down a completely different path. Living on a ranch would probably drive her crazy in short order.

As he huddled in the dank cave, filled with tenderness and love for the woman in his arms, the same question kept taunting him.

Why, Lord, why have You brought her into my life?

Shannon had fallen asleep, and he was grateful for it. The responsibility of keeping her safe was a heavy one. She had risen with unbelievable determination to every challenge the hard climb had thrown at her. A woman conditioned to the altitude and vigorous physical demands couldn't have done any better. He hated to think of leaving her here alone, but he had to get a radio message to McGrady and check on the crash site. There was no question about it. Getting to the injured Pete as soon as possible was imperative.

Adding up all the information Ross had told him, Ward was pretty sure he had mentally zeroed in on the likely place where the helicopter had gone down. Ward reasoned that all he had to do was retrace his steps to the place where they had found Ross, then head for the deep ravine that lay almost in a direct line with the waterfall.

From time to time he glanced out the mine's entrance. Was the rain slacking off? Was it just hopeful thinking? He waited a few minutes more, then was sure—the echo of thunder was getting fainter. Good. That meant that interference from lightning might have lessened enough for him to make a radio transmission. He gently removed his arms from around Shannon.

She woke up with a start. For a moment, her eyes rounded in confusion. Where am I? Then she remembered. "What's the matter? What's happened?"

"Nothing. It's okay. You've been sleeping." He brushed a kiss on top of her damp head. "Sorry to wake you up, but I think the storm may be about over."

"It's still raining," she protested as she glanced out the tunnel's opening.

"I know, but it's slacking off. Listen. You can tell the thunder is moving farther away. Maybe I can get a radio transmission through now." He eased away from her, stood up and took the radio from the case fastened to his belt.

Hope spurted through her as he stepped outside into a light rain shower. Shielding the radio with his face and cowboy hat, he turned one way and then another. She couldn't tell whether he was talking because she couldn't see his lips clearly.

Maybe…maybe…?

She held her breath. If he could report where they were, all they had to do was sit and wait for a rescue team. When he strode into the tunnel, her hopes were dashed.

He shook his head. "The transmission keeps breaking up. There's still too much electrical interference. I'll have to keep trying, but before I leave—?"

"Leave? What do you mean, leave?" She jerked to her feet.

He put his hands on her shoulders looked straight into her frightened eyes and explained that he wanted to resume his search for the helicopter.

"But it's still raining! It's insanity for you to even think about going out in this weather." Her voice trembled in utter disbelief.

"The storm is moving on, and the rain is slacking off. I'm hoping it will stop altogether before night sets in."

"You don't even know where the copter went down."

"I have a pretty good idea. There are a few hours of daylight left. I'm going to check it out, and I'll keep trying to contact McGrady."

You can't leave me here alone!

Even as the frantic plea crossed her mind, she knew it was exactly what he intended to do. She also knew that pleading with him would be a waste of breath. One thing she knew without any doubt, Ward Dawson was his own man, and he wouldn't be swayed from doing what he thought was right. She wanted to insist on going with him, but that was out of the question. She knew it, and so did he.

He started unloading his backpack. "I'll leave the sandwiches I packed, the canteen, a couple of apples, a flashlight and matches. Once the rain stops, you can build a fire." He started to ask if she'd ever built a bonfire, but he knew the answer from her expression. "Here's a map to use as paper. Just make sure the fire is close enough to the entrance to let the smoke out. Understand?" She nodded, but she really wasn't taking in any of what he was saying. The thought of being left alone in this abandoned mine was bad enough, but what about the injured pilot?

"What about...about Ross?" she stammered anxiously. *What if he gets worse? What if he dies?*

"His breathing and heartbeat are still regular," Ward reassured her. "He'll probably stay asleep, for a while at least. When he wakes up, give him some water and see if he wants to eat anything. There's a little of our lunch left."

"When will you be back?"

"I don't know. But you can handle this, Shannon. I know you can."

She knew it was useless to argue. Her head came up. "Please, take care of yourself. I don't want to have to come looking for you."

He chuckled and gave her a tender look as if he were going to say something more, then he turned and was gone.

Weird shadows that seemed alive began to invade the mine tunnel as it became darker outside. At first, as the hours crept by, she kept her eyes on the mine's entrance, wanting to see Ward's returning figure. Surely, he would decide he'd been wrong about the storm blowing over. He would come back, and they would wait for morning together.

The fantasy faded as the rain slowed to a trickle and night shadows crept into the already dark abyss of the mine. She steeled herself to wait out the night in silence alone when suddenly Ross moaned and started thrashing out at the poncho that covered him. Shannon quickly bent over him, using the flashlight to see his face.

"Ross, are you awake?" His eyes were open, but they had a frightened glazed look about them. With her free hand, she felt his forehead. She silently groaned.

No wonder he was flinging off everything. He had a fever.

"Water," he croaked.

"Yes, water." She grabbed the canteen, lifted his head and let him take a deep swallow. Her mind raced. What should she do? What did she know about fevers? She'd had the flu a couple of winters ago. What had she done for the fever? Aspirin and plenty of water.

She grabbed the first aid kit Ward had left and was all thumbs as she gave him two of the pills and enough water to swallow them.

"You'll feel better now," she promised him with false bravado in her voice.

"Pete?" He tried to sit up.

"Ward is looking for him now. We just have to wait." She bit her lip as she added silently, *And wait, and wait.*

As the hours passed, strange noises from the depths of the mine brought a new fear. As she huddled in the darkness with the injured man, her imagination taunted her. Was some wild night creature beginning to move? Maybe the mine was filled with bats. The thought sent a cold prickling up her spine.

As a young child she'd been frightened many times when her parents left her alone for most of the night while they partied with friends in another apartment. She'd wake up in the middle of the night, listening to the frightening noises and knowing they hadn't come home.

Maybe they wouldn't. Maybe she'd be all alone forever. She'd lay awake for hours, stiff and frightened, waiting to hear the sound of their muffled laughter as they passed her room. She never called out to them, fearing they would chide her for being a baby. Above everything else, she wanted their approval, and the fear had never left her that they wouldn't love her if she didn't measure up.

As she sat there alone, childish memories she had buried deep became real again. The light of her flashlight began to dim, and in a few minutes the batteries went dead. As the darkness closed in, she fought the driving need to get to her feet and run. She felt all alone again. Uncertain and fearful. The strong confidence she'd struggled to maintain all her life deserted her. She felt totally helpless. The driving forces in her life, prestige and money, were valueless in the circumstances. There was nothing she could do for the man who might be dying just feet away. Nothing, she could do for herself.

You could pray. Ward's voice was as clear as if he'd been whispering in her ear.

She jerked her head up and searched the empty shadowy darkness.

"I don't know how," she answered, as if he were there to hear.

Yes, you do.

"No, I don't."

Try.

She'd listened to the prayers others had spoken during the evening prayer gatherings at the ranch, but she had always remained silent. Ward had assured her that prayers were just like communicating with a beloved friend. As she sat there, cold and fearful, she knew she'd never needed a friend more.

She moistened her lips. Not knowing how to start, she repeated one of the verses that seemed to be a favorite with everyone.

Call upon the Lord and He will give you the desires of your heart.

Drawing upon that promise, she began to put into words all the feelings that were swelling up inside her. "I thought I could handle anything, but now I know I can't. Please help me get through this. I've never thought I needed to believe in anything but my own determination and my own strong will." For the first time, she admitted an honesty that stripped away the worldly pretenses that had been the guiding force in her life. Her driving ambition seemed hollow and barren. "I need to change. I know that," she whispered. "God, please help me. Don't let Ross die. Bring Ward back safely." Not knowing what to do or say next, she whispered a faint, "Amen."

Putting her head against her drawn-up knees, she fell silent. She didn't feel any different after offering her stumbling prayer. In fact there was a faint mockery deep inside that she'd offered up her fears to a God she'd never known before.

"Water," Ross croaked in a dry voice.

She fumbled in the shadowy darkness until she found the canteen. Then she helped him sit up while he drank. She couldn't see his face well enough to know if he was fully conscious, but she was relieved when he remained seated.

"Feeling better?" she asked hopefully.

"I don't hear any thunder," he mumbled.

"The storm is just about over. It's stopped raining."

"That's good. They'll find Pete now."

"Yes," she replied in a positive tone that didn't match her apprehension.

Where was Ward? Had he reached the helicopter safely? And what had he found?

"I'm sorry," he said as they sat in the dark.

"Nothing to be sorry about," she reassured him. "You've shown a lot of courage, Ross. You could have stayed in the helicopter, but you didn't. You went for help."

"And ended up here?" he asked, as if he was trying to reassure himself that this dark hole in the ground was for real.

"It was the only place out of the rain. I just wish there was something I could do to make you more comfortable." She was relieved that he seemed stronger and more lucid than before. Having someone to talk with made all the difference in the world in her feelings. The sound of their voices echoing in the tunnel was reassuring and comforting.

"You're a brave lady, Miss—"

"Shannon."

"Why don't you take this?" He started to give her the poncho. "I'm not very cold. I was just dreaming that I was sitting in front of a fire."

Shannon smiled, wondering if Ross had overheard what Ward had told her about using her imagination to keep warm. "No, you keep it around you." She felt his forehead. "I do think your fever has gone down."

She glanced out the mine opening. Was it safe to have a fire? The next question was, could she build one? Her expertise in this area was sadly lacking. Gas fireplaces didn't require anything more than turning a switch. She'd never laid a fire.

So what? some inner voice chided her. You've done a lot of things in your life for the first time. Shannon tried to remember what instructions Ward had given her. At the time, her thoughts had been reeling with the shock that he was going to leave her, and she hadn't focused on what he was saying.

Close to the entrance. Use the map for paper.

"Yes, I think I'll build us a nice, warm fire," she said with more confidence than she felt. "Ward collected some wood and left some matches. It shouldn't be that hard." She was talking to herself more than to Ross.

"It isn't," Ross said in a stronger voice than she'd heard before. "You just have to start out right. That's what I tell my Cub Scouts. You need to use small pieces of wood at first."

"All right. Let's give it a try."

Ward had left the pile of wood just inside the mouth of the tunnel. Shannon lingered for a moment at the entrance, gratefully breathing in the fresh night air. Everything glistened with droplets of water, and in the shimmering patina of moonlight, the landscape looked like a painting dipped in silver. She had never seen anything so beautiful. Never again would she take the spacious out-of-doors for granted.

Ross suddenly came up behind her with shuffling labored steps, then eased down on the ground. "Let's build that fire, Shannon."

Following his instructions, she used the map and small pieces of wood to form a kind of teepee. Then she carefully lit a match. Her hand was so shaky the first two matches went out before she could light the paper. The third try was a success.

"That's it," Ross said. "Now feed more wood to the blaze when it gets a little bigger. Don't put on too much wood too fast or you'll suffocate it. Good job, Shannon," Ross said a little while later when dancing flames licked at the old dry wood and gave out a blessed circle of warmth.

"Maybe I could get the hang of this camping thing, after all," Shannon said, surprised at the satisfaction she felt sitting beside a fire she'd built with her own hands. Her spirits were almost light as she looked at the heavens, where stars twinkled at her through thinning clouds.

"Ward was right, you know," Ross said thoughtfully.

"About what?"

"When I said that it was luck that led me to that exact spot where you found me, Ward corrected me. Not luck, but divine guidance." Ross was silent for a moment, then added, "The good Lord answers our prayers in strange ways sometimes."

"He certainly does," she answered thoughtfully. She no longer felt alone and was strangely at peace.

Was God answering her prayers?

Chapter Fourteen

Shannon and Ross passed the night talking and confessing things about themselves they probably wouldn't have under any other conditions. From time to time, they dozed off as they sat leaning against the outside of the tunnel.

When dawn came, Shannon fed the last piece of wood to the fire. For breakfast, they shared the apple and sandwich Ward had left, and finished the last of the water in the canteen. Shannon didn't trust herself to find her way to the waterfall because she had become disoriented in the rain. She regretted not taking any food from the hamper when she had dashed after Ward.

"They should be coming after us before long," Ross sighed as they watched the sun getting higher and higher.

"Yes," Shannon hopefully agreed. If Ward got through to McGrady last night, the rescue team could be on its way by now.

She knew Ross was hurting. He looked awful in the daylight with matted blood on his face and clothes.

"Are you all right? Do you hurt anywhere?"

"Only all over," he answered with a wry grin. "Nothing serious."

She knew he was making light of his condition. His courage and companionship had give her the strength she needed to get through the night, and she was deeply grateful to him.

Hurry, Ward, please hurry.

As the morning hours passed, Ross sat quietly in the warming sun, but Shannon's restlessness grew. She began walking back and forth in front of the mine, her eyes searching the surrounding terrain. Several times she stopped and listened.

Nothing.

When her ears picked up the faint sound of men's voices, she was afraid to believe it was true. She froze like a statue, waiting, holding her breath until three men came into view a short distance below the mine.

Ross saw them at the same time, and he gave a weak shout, "Hurrah."

Shannon's eyes instantly flew to the figure walking behind the two uniformed men. Ward! With a joyful cry, she darted forward, slipping and sliding all the way down the muddy incline. When she reached him, she threw herself in his arms and unabashedly hugged and kissed him.

"Wow." One of the young men laughed. "What I wouldn't do for a greeting like that."

Ward responded to her welcome with a fervor of his own. His hands pressed her close, and he let his mouth trail from her mouth to the sweet softness of her cheek. The torment of leaving her alone instantly faded. She radiated a new confidence. Even with her hair hanging listless around her smudged face, her clothes soiled and wrinkled, she was beautiful. And the way her shining eyes were looking at him filled him with incredible happiness. She had been in his prayers during the long night he had held his vigil in the wreckage of the helicopter. He didn't know what had happened while he'd been gone, but there was something different about the way she was keeping her arm possessively around him.

She was all right! *Thank you, Lord.* And from the way Ross was standing waiting for them to reach him, he was all right, too.

Ross called out before they reached him. "Pete? What about Pete?"

"The rescue helicopter lifted him off about an hour ago. I spent the night with him. He's got some broken bones, but they say his vital signs are good."

"What about you, fellow?" asked one of the paramedics as they stopped beside Ross.

"I'm okay."

"You two guys are one lucky pair of dudes," a young, curly-haired paramedic told Ross. "How either of you survived that crash is a miracle."

"We sure didn't expect to find you looking this good," the older attendant added.

"I had a good nurse." Ross smiled at Shannon.

"Well, we need to give you the once-over. Make sure we don't need a stretcher to get back to where the helicopter can pick you up later."

While the two attendants bent over Ross, Shannon

and Ward walked a little distance away. They still had their arms around each other as if afraid to let go.

"I don't believe it," Ward said, smiling at her. "What kind of nursing went on while I was gone? I expected to find Ross flat out, unconscious. What happened?"

For some reason, she wasn't ready to confess her feeble attempt to pray. She didn't want him to jump to the conclusion that she had become something she wasn't. One prayer didn't make her a devout Christian. Certainly not the dedicated kind of woman he was looking for. "I don't know."

He knew she was holding something back, but he didn't press her. He'd wait for a better time to share the long tedious night that had just passed. They both were exhausted, mentally and physically.

After the paramedics examined Ross, they were satisfied he had not suffered any broken bones or internal injuries and were prepared to take him to the place where the returning helicopter would set down. A portable stretcher was ready if the hike proved too much.

Impulsively, Shannon gave Ross a hug as they were ready to leave the mine. "Thank you. Take care," she whispered as a hint of tears collected in her eyes.

"You, too." His eyes were misty.

Ward and Shannon watched them leave, then he asked, "Ready for a hike back to the Jeep?"

"I've never been more ready," she answered. As they walked away from the mine, she took a deep breath of the fresh pine-scented air and lifted her face to the warmth of the sun. "It's a beautiful day."

"The day after a storm is always uplifting. Everything looks fresh and new. Makes you feel great to be alive, doesn't it?''

"Yes, but I'm not sure I'm ready to face a long hike," she admitted honestly. Already the blister on her heel was beginning to hurt. Thankfully, she soon discovered that going down the mountainside was certainly less demanding than climbing up the rocky slopes.

"We can take our time," Ward assured her. "When I finally got through to Chief McGrady last night, I asked him to get a message to Beth that we were spending the night. I didn't want her and Tara to worry."

The Jeep was just where they had left it, and so was the hamper of food Beth had packed. Although eating had not been at the front of Shannon's mind during the last twenty-four hours, as they sat in the Jeep, her appetite came back.

"Feeling better?" he asked, secretly amused at her obvious enjoyment of the day-old food.

"Much."

"Nothing like food, sunshine and a successful mission to put the world right."

She didn't answer, and he could see her forehead furrowed in thought. Suddenly she turned in the seat to face him. "Last night, Ross said you were right...about it not being luck that we found him. He also said that sometimes God doesn't answer our prayers the way we expect. Is that right?"

He nodded and smiled. "Do you want to hear a story that makes that point? There was this guy who got lost in Alaska. He was all alone, didn't know where he was, nothing but ice and snow stretching out in every direction, and he prayed to God to save him. The poor guy was about to freeze to death when an Inuit showed up and took him back to civilization.''

Shannon looked at him, puzzled. ''So?''

''Well, when someone asked the man what had happened, he told them how he'd been lost and almost died. 'I prayed to God to save me,' he said indignantly, 'but He didn't do anything. If that Inuit hadn't shown up, I'd have frozen to death.''' Ward chuckled. ''God uses anyone or anything that's handy to perform His blessings.''

''I see,'' she said thoughtfully. She hesitated to tell him about asking for God's help last night. She needed time to understand what had happened—if anything. Certainly, no Inuit had showed up to offer her help.

What about Ross?

Ward's story suddenly put everything in a different light as she thought about what had happened last night. When Ross got better and began to interact with her, her panic at being alone had almost instantly dissipated. She'd never expected the injured pilot to recover so quickly and become a companion in the terrifying situation—but he had! A comradeship had developed between them, and his presence had strengthened her through the long night hours.

Had the injured Ross been her Inuit? God's answer to her prayer?

Ward watched her, not knowing why she was worrying her lip as she seemed to be fighting some invisible challenge. ''Do you want to tell me about it?''

She shook her head.

He stifled his disappointment. Every time he thought

they were getting closer to sharing soul-searching feelings with each other, she backed off.

"I need to do some thinking first," she said. Above everything else, she wanted to be honest with Ward and herself. She didn't want to make promises she might not be able to keep.

As they headed to the ranch, the narrow Jeep road was even more treacherous than before. The drive up the mountain had been grueling, but coming down was worse. Yesterday's heavy rain had washed earth and rocks down the mountain slopes, and in some spots Ward had to maneuver the Jeep's wheels cautiously over the accumulated mud and rocks.

When they finally reached the paved road running along the river, Ward loosened the knuckle-white grip he had on the steering wheel. "We're almost home."

Home. The word had a nice sound to it, Shannon thought, even though it didn't quite seem to apply in the present situation. She was too weary at the moment to handle any emotional analysis.

Ward sounded the horn as he stopped the Jeep at the back of the house. The kitchen door flew open. Wiping her hands on her apron, Beth hurried out.

As Ward and Shannon wearily climbed out, she gasped, "Heaven help us. You two look like death warmed over."

"I guess we feel like it, too," Ward admitted with a tired grin as Tara bounded out of the house with Pokey at her heels.

"Daddy, Daddy. You're back." She threw herself at him. "Where did you go? Why didn't you take me?"

As he lifted his daughter up for a big hug, weariness

eased out of him, and he felt renewed. The demanding experience he'd been through made him realize once again how precious life is. Not one minute of love should be wasted.

"Yes, I'm back." He laughed. "And how's my little cowpoke?"

"I'm all better now," Tara said. "And my hair is going to grow back. Aunt Beth said so."

Shannon could see that one of Tara's pigtails was a little thin, and she still wore a small bandage on her head, but her dancing eyes and broad grin were the same. Warm feelings spilled through Shannon as she watched Ward unabashedly show his deep love for his daughter. That's what fathers and daughters should feel for each other, she thought. Unconditional love wasn't about money or pride.

As soon as Ward put Tara down, she ran to Shannon, and grabbed her hand. "Come see Princess. She's all bigger."

"In one day?" Shannon teased. "That's all I've been gone."

"It seems longer," Tara insisted.

"Yes, it does." How wise children were, Shannon thought. Sometimes time couldn't be measured in minutes. A lifetime could pass in a few hours—or in one long night.

"Tara, can't you see these two are dead on their feet?" Beth chided. "Goodness gracious, I've seen half-plucked chickens in better shape."

Ward laughed. "That's what I like about you, Sis. You're not a bit shy about calling things as you see them."

"Well, anyone with eyes in their head can tell you're both on your last legs." She sobered. "We were all worried about you being out in that thunderstorm. It hit here with the force of a gale. The whole house shook as if it might be lifted off its rock foundation. The windows rattled, loose tiles flew off the roof, and the trees in the yard were almost bent double."

"You should have been here," Tara said with child-like enthusiasm. "Kenny and I ran around the house, singing, 'It's raining, it's pouring, the old man is snoring.' But Kenny's grandpa laughed and shook his finger at us. 'I am not snoring.'" She giggled. "We kept singing, anyway."

"That's enough, Tara," Beth said briskly. "You can tell them your stories later, and from what Chief McGrady said to me, these two have a few to tell us."

"Is Ted still at his grandmother's place?" Ward asked.

Beth nodded. "As far as I know."

"Then I'd better check on the horses and the ranch hands." With Tara tagging along, he headed toward the stables.

Beth motioned to Shannon. "Come on, honey, let's get you cleaned up and into a nice warm bed."

It was heavenly having someone take charge. Shannon meekly let Beth run a bath, then settle her in her own bed instead of the cot Shannon had been using. Having someone fuss over her had been a rare experience, even as a child.

"Have a nice long nap. I'll have a nice meal ready for you when you wake up."

"You're too good to everyone, Beth," Shannon told

her, marveling at the way Beth gave of herself in so many ways.

"Nonsense," Beth scoffed with her usual briskness. "I haven't seen any sign of a halo the last time I looked in the mirror."

Shannon moistened her lips. "Do you...do you think God always answers prayers?"

"Yes," Beth nodded readily. "Why are you smiling?"

Shannon was too tired to explain about Inuits. She closed her eyes and was hardly aware of the bedroom door quietly closing.

When Shannon awoke five hours later, it was dark. She could hear muffled sounds in the house, and smelled tantalizing smells wafting from the kitchen. Suddenly she was ravenous and filled with a sense of excitement. How wonderful to be part of a bustling household!

Quickly dressing in the new outfit she'd bought in Elkhorn, she hurried downstairs. The television was blaring, and people had collected in the small sitting room, listening to a newscaster.

"Only a few warm spots remain after the deluge of rain," he reported. "Most of the firefighters and National Guard are pulling out, leaving only a small number of men to clean up. The crisis is over."

"Yahoo."

"Hurrah!"

"Praise God."

"The fire's over. The fire's over." Tara, Kenny and

Gloria grabbed hands and began dancing around the room. Pokey bounded at their heels, barking.

The adults hugged each other.

Ward reached for Shannon, and she leaned into the length of his strong body with a joy she wouldn't have thought possible. His lips lightly touched her ear. "Time to celebrate."

She closed her eyes and shoved away all unanswered questions about her future. All that mattered at the moment was that the nightmare was over.

"All persons evacuated from their homes are asked to report to the center tomorrow morning," the newscaster continued. "Arrangements will be made to conduct groups into the affected areas for an assessment of property damage."

"Does that mean we'll be going back home?" Kenny asked eagerly.

His parents looked at each other, and his father answered cautiously, "We'll have to wait and see, Kenny. They're saying that some of the homes in our area have been spared. Maybe ours is one of them."

Mr. Winters spoke. "Hazel and I have decided that no matter what we find, we'll move to Arizona to be close to our daughter and grandchildren. An experience like this makes us realize that family is the most important thing in life." The gray-haired couple smiled at each other. "We've not seen nearly enough of ours in the last few years. It's time to make up for lost time."

Gloria's parents were pointedly quiet, and Shannon suspected they were putting off making any decisions until they knew whether their home had been reduced to smoldering rubble or was still standing.

All of them thanked Ward and Beth for their hospitality, and there were a few tears shed as they expressed their gratitude.

"Come on, everybody. Into the dining room," Beth ordered with a wave of her hand. "We're going to have ourselves a thanksgiving feast."

In a matter of minutes, the dining room table was loaded. Shannon couldn't believe how much food Beth had set out. Everyone teased her about having a magic wand to produce such a feast on short notice.

Beth laughed and admitted she had raided her freezer. "What better time to enjoy God's bounty?" Then she added with her usual practical honesty, "It was getting too full anyway. My garden will be going crazy with all this rain."

There was room for everyone around the large oval table, and even Kenny's grandfather parked his wheelchair with the others. Ward made sure Shannon sat next to him.

After he gave a sincere lengthy blessing, the level of talk and laughter rose like helium balloons. The tension of the last weeks gave way to a thankful joy.

Ward teased Shannon about preferring egg sandwiches to fried chicken. As they laughed at their private joke, Ward couldn't believe how much she had changed from the woman he had met. Gone was the chilly, stuck-up manner that had challenged him the first time he stopped her car. Her whole demeanor had softened. Her eyes had lost their hard glint and her lovely mouth its rigidity.

As he watched Shannon laugh and joke with the others, he knew she was looking at people and life in a different way than before. On the ride back, he had sensed a tenuous surrender to a belief in God, and he wanted to think her priorities had changed.

But had they?

Because of the traumatic events that had affected her life, she seemed to be content to sit at his table and enjoy the simple food, talk and laughter. But would it last? How could the humdrum of a rancher's life compete with the excitement of being a career woman in a big city? She had changed—but maybe not that much.

She was obviously embarrassed when Kenny's grandfather leaned toward her and asked in his cracking voice, "Don't you want to draw another picture of me? My son says you're wasting good talent."

"Dad!" Tom Gordon protested. "I just said she had a lot of ability she wasn't using."

"Isn't that the same thing?" the old man muttered. Then he turned his attention to his glass of milk, as if bored with the conversation.

"Have you done any more sketches while you've been here?" Tom asked, trying to cover for his father.

"A few. Mostly just sketches to entertain the children."

"Some of these mountain scenes would look great on greeting cards. And horses are always a good subject."

"You could draw Princess and Calico," Tara offered, jumping into the conversation.

"I'll think about it," Shannon said, surprised when she felt a quiver of excitement talking about the possibility that maybe, just maybe, she might take up drawing in earnest sometime.

"You could give me a picture of Princess for my birthday," Tara said with a bright smile.

"Oh, and when is that?" When Tara told her the date, she smiled. "That's not very far away."

"I know. You can come to my birthday party and everything. I'm wishing for something special for my birthday," Tara said, her eyes glistening. "Do you want to know what it is?"

"If you want to tell me."

"I'm wishing for a new mommy." The little girl grinned at Shannon with a knowing far beyond her years. "Do you think my daddy will get me one?"

All the table conversation came to an abrupt stop as everyone's eyes fell on Shannon and Ward. For a brief moment, the silence was deafening. Then everyone started speaking at once as if trying to cover up the embarrassment.

Beth pushed back her chair. "Anyone for dessert?"

Shannon kept her eyes lowered. She couldn't bear to look at Ward. There were too many things unsettled between them.

Chapter Fifteen

Although Ward had tried to make light of Tara's announcement, the flush on his face made it clear that he was embarrassed by it.

When everyone began to collect in the sitting room for evening prayers, Shannon quietly excused herself. Ward walked with her to the bottom of the stairs.

"I'm terribly sorry. Not for the world would I have had you embarrassed like that," he apologized.

"You can't fault Tara for being up-front and speaking her mind." She hadn't intended for it to sound like a criticism, but it came out that way.

"You're right. We need to talk about this."

"Yes, but not tonight."

"The timing isn't good is it?"

"No, it isn't," she said firmly. She didn't like the idea that he was being forced into declaring his intentions by the innocent remarks of a little girl. "Now that the emergency is over, we all need to look at things more clearly."

More clearly. Her brisk, businesslike tone was not lost on Ward. Her protective barriers had gone up again, and he upbraided himself for letting it happen. They had been drawing closer every day they spent together, and now all that was being lost because of bad timing on his part for not speaking sooner.

At that inopportune moment, Beth poked her head out of the sitting room. "We're waiting, Ward. Aren't you two coming?"

"In a minute."

Shannon quickly said good-night and didn't look at him as she mounted the stairs. She prepared for bed as if she wasn't slowly breaking to pieces inside.

Where was this attraction between them going to lead? Why didn't he declare himself?

All her life she'd made plans and meticulous preparations for what lay ahead, but at the moment she was floundering like a boat without a rudder. How could she plan a future when she didn't even understand the present?

As she lay rigid in her tiny bed, something Beth had said came back to her. "Trust in the Lord and He will direct your path."

Trust. Shannon had turned the word over in her mind, and then had shaken her head. "I'm not sure I'm ready to give up my driver's seat, Beth."

I'm still not sure, Shannon admitted as she lay awake despite a lingering bone-deep weariness. She knew she loved Ward with a depth that she'd never felt for anyone, but she had only dipped her toes in the waters of becoming a Christian. For good reason, Ward might not believe it was lasting. A lot of people made promises to God under stress, then slipped back into their own way of thinking. How could she be sure she wasn't one of them? It wasn't fair to Ward to pretend she had experienced a deep conversion when her faith was about as solid as a soap bubble.

She pretended to be asleep when Beth came to bed, but she could hear the soft whisper of her nightly prayers, and somehow, even secondhand, they had a soothing effect. Silently, Shannon said her own, amen and fell asleep.

Breakfast was a hurried affair. A hopeful excitement put a smile on everyone's face. There were plenty of hugs and thank-yous to go around as the families made preparations to leave the ranch and return to the evacuation center.

Ward was pleased when Shannon smiled at him without any hint of last night's unpleasantness. She looked relaxed and rested. He couldn't keep his eyes off her. He impulsively put his arm around her waist and kissed her cheek. She smelled wonderful, and the softness of her skin stayed on his lips as he looked at her. If there had been any music at all, he would have danced her right around the kitchen floor.

"Sleep well?" he asked, locking his eyes with hers.

"Actually, I did."

"Good. Ted brought the truck back last night, so you and Tara can ride with me into the Junction."

"I hadn't planned on going. I'll stay here and help Beth straighten up."

"You'll do nothing of the sort," Beth intervened in her no-nonsense voice. "I'm looking forward to having the place all to myself. Besides, they'll be needing some extra hands at the school. I'm thinking there's going to be plenty of heartaches and disappointments when some folks get bad news.''

"I'm afraid you're right,'' Ward agreed. Who knew what the families would find left on the scorched mountainsides? "Well, let's get going, folks.''

After all the others had left in their cars, Ward and Shannon climbed in the truck Ted had exchanged for his Jeep. Ted's grandmother had decided to stay in her home since the fire danger was over.

Shannon was thankful for Tara sitting between them, chatting away with her usual exuberance. "Kenny said he'd bring Pokey back to see me, Daddy. And I told him he could come and pet Princess any time he wanted. Isn't that super-duper?''

Ward smiled at his daughter. "Sounds super-duper to me.''

"Why did it take so long for God to make it rain?'' Tara asked, her mind hopping to another subject.

"His time is not our time,'' Ward answered easily. "And maybe there were lessons to be learned.''

"And some of us are slow learners,'' Shannon offered with a rueful smile as her eyes connected with Ward's.

"Not me,'' Tara said. "I learn quickly, don't I, Daddy?''

"Sometimes too quick.'' Ward gave Shannon a conspirator's wink over the little girl's head that drew them together in a strange way—like an intimate bond between the three of them.

As they drove into Beaver Junction, an air of excitement was everywhere in the small community. Streets and sidewalks were filled with people moving about with new energy and optimism. Although the main road out of the Junction was still closed to general traffic, numerous fire units had already left their fighting positions, and convoys were moving out of the area.

The area around the school resembled the bustle of an anthill. Several television crews were busily panning the crowd and looking for stories. At the entrance to the school, Red Cross workers were on full alert, acting as dispatchers for the vans arriving at the school to drive families into the burned-out areas. A loudspeaker announced that after surveying their property, the families would be brought back to the evacuation center until emergency traffic was thin enough to allow personal cars on the narrow roads.

"I'll take Beth's garden produce to the kitchen," Shannon offered as they joined the crowd pushing into the school. "Tara can go with me."

Ward nodded. "I'm going to see if they need more drivers. Will you be all right if I get tied up for a few hours?"

"We'll be fine, won't we, Tara?"

"Hunky-dorky." She giggled. "That's what Kenny always says." Ward sent her a warning look. "Just make sure that everything stays hunky-dorky. Don't give Shannon any trouble."

"I won't, Daddy. I'll be real good."

Ward watched as Tara took Shannon's free hand and hugged her side as they walked away.

If she leaves us, Tara, what will we do?

* * *

As Shannon and Tara made their way across the crowded gym, a rush of memories came to Shannon. Memories that clashed with the present moment. She remembered how she sat in the corner, alone, resentful and angry at the inconvenience the wildfire had caused. As far as she was concerned the whole situation had been simply something to be endured. How could she have known the experience was going to change her whole life? She looked at Tara holding her hand and she was grateful her life had been touched by this child's love. All the discomfort she had experienced these past weeks was worth one smile from this little girl.

When they reached the kitchen, Laura was there, as usual, busy as three people. It seemed to Shannon that the cafeteria was more crowded and hectic than ever.

"Well, look who's here." Laura gave Shannon and Tara her usual ready smile. "What's this I hear, Shannon, about you and Ward rescuing a couple of pilots? Word is that they both owe their lives to you."

"Not me. It was Ward who did the rescuing." Shannon quickly corrected Laura.

"Well, I want to hear all about it some time. I'm betting you have a story of your own to tell."

The invitation to share her frightened surrender to prayer with Laura was tempting, but Shannon was afraid Laura would read too much into it. "Maybe sometime," she said vaguely.

"Good. We're having a short worship service in a few minutes. I was just about ready to head in that direction." With her usual easy commanding manner, she took Shannon and Tara in tow, and they made their way through the crowded gym.

She gave Shannon a promising smile when they reached the auditorium. "See you after service. I've got a few things to tend to. Preacher's wife, you know."

Almost immediately, Tara saw Kenny and Gloria near the front and bounded over to sit with them. Shannon hesitated to join them. Instead she took a seat near the back. Familiar sights, smells and sounds triggered a flood of memories of that Sunday morning she'd been there with Ward. How vividly she remembered the way he had smiled at her, ignoring how she shifted uncomfortably in her seat during the service. Even now, she could hear his deep clear voice raised in song and feel the warmth of his large hand as it tenderly engulfed hers, giving her reassurance.

Every time someone came through the door behind her, she turned hopefully. Maybe... But she was disappointed. Obviously there had been a need for Ward's services somewhere else, or he would have been back.

She was ashamed when she remembered how she had behaved toward him in the beginning. Why had he bothered to befriend her? What had he seen in her that made him willing to take her into his home? Would it be enough for any future they might have together?

The worship service was one of jubilation and thanksgiving. Reverend Cozzins's message reminded them of the good things that had happened in the midst of the tragedy—people had been drawn closer together, there were more displays of kindness and generosity than before, there was a realization of what was important in life.

"All of us have been changed by this experience. We need to look ahead, not back."

Shannon bowed her head as Reverend Cozzins prayed that the lessons of the wildfires would not be forgotten, and in her heart she echoed that prayer. She was surprised by the feeling of surrender that came over her. When the minister read Jeremiah 29:11, it seemed that the scripture was directed right at her.

"'For I know the plans I have for you,' declares the Lord. 'Plans to prosper you, and not to harm you. Plans to give you a hope and a future.'"

The words echoed in her heart. *A future and a hope.* Ward had told her there was a divine plan for every child of God, and now she believed him. Why else was she sitting in this place feeling totally complete for the first time in her life?

After the service was over, people hugged and smiled at each other, and differences that might have been between them before the wildfire had faded in the life-and-death situation they had faced. Why did it take a catastrophe to bring out the best in human nature? Shannon wondered.

She collected Tara, and they made their way out of the auditorium with the rest of the crowd. Shannon was surprised when Judy came up to her and asked about Ward.

"He's helping out somewhere," Shannon told her.

"I've been worried about him," she said. "He doesn't use good judgment sometimes."

"I'm sure he can take care of himself," Shannon

answered, wondering where this conversation was going.

"He always has, up until now. But sometimes men get a little off balance, you know what I mean?"

"No, I'm not sure that I do," Shannon answered. "Ward seems to be about the most balanced man I've ever met."

"Really. I would have thought you'd be bored to death with a plain old cowboy. It's too bad your vacation turned out to be such a bummer. I guess you'll be leaving soon?"

"No," Tara said, glaring at Judy. "Shannon's not leaving. She's staying."

"Not even to go back to California where she lives?" Judy asked in the patronizing tone adults often use with children. "I bet she's ready to get out of here and get back to where all the action is."

"My daddy isn't going to let Shannon go away," Tara declared, giving a pugnacious lift to her little chin. "Besides, we're all going there to see Disneyland, Hollywood and Sea World. Aren't we, Shannon?"

The lie was a whopper, but Shannon wasn't about to let Tara down. "Yes, we are."

"Well, I guess that answers my question."

Shannon knew Judy's assumption was premature. No matter how much Tara liked her, Ward would never allow himself to be manipulated by his daughter.

Judy turned her back on them and walked away with a decided slump to her slender shoulders.

Tara kept close to Shannon's side as they made their way to the cafeteria. Lunch was a hurried affair with people coming and going as if the school had suddenly turned into a bus station.

Evacuated families anxiously waited for their scheduled time slot to tour their home. The vans began leaving the school. Mr. and Mrs. Winters and Gloria's parents were in the first group. Shannon could tell from their worried expressions that they feared the worst.

Shannon was surprised when a Red Cross volunteer came up to her. "Miss Hensley?" At Shannon's nod, the woman studied her clipboard. "Your name is on the list of people living on Prospect Mountain."

"I was renting a place there," Shannon acknowledged.

"We have a van going to that area at two o'clock. You will be able to view the damage, but you will not be allowed to stay in the area until the okay is given for you to return."

Shannon's first impulse was to decline the offer to see whether or not the rented cottage still stood. She wasn't quite sure why she nodded at the lady and said, "Thank you." Perhaps she needed some kind of closure to the events that had stripped her of car and possessions, her false pride and even her direction in life.

As Shannon and Tara waited for their ride, they were surprised to find that Kenny and his parents were going in the same group. When the van pulled up in front of the school, Shannon had an even bigger surprise. Ward was the driver.

Tara squealed, dashed into the van, and gave him a hug. "I'm going to sit with Kenny," she announced, and bounded toward the back of the van.

"Never saw a bus driver in a cowboy hat before," Shannon teased as she took a front seat.

"Yep, we're pretty versatile, ma'am." The corners of his mouth quirked with a grin. "Come rain or shine, I'm your man."

The double meaning brought a warmth to her face. "But can you drive these mountain roads?" she asked with mock seriousness.

"I reckon I can give it a try. I've had a little experience."

"Really? I never would have guessed."

His smile faded a little. "It may not be a very pretty ride. Are you sure you want to go?"

"Yes," she said firmly. "I need to see it."

He nodded. "I understand."

Shannon wasn't sure she did, but she wanted to witness the devastation with her own eyes. In some strange way she needed to see the charred trees and scorched earth and smell the lingering acrid smoke. There was an undefined need to find assurance in her heart that in time the mountain would heal itself. It surprised her how deeply she had come to love these rugged surroundings. If she'd been born here, being the kind of wife Ward deserved would have come naturally to her.

They left the school, drove through Beaver Junction and headed up the mountain road that had been opened to official travel. Ward chuckled when they passed the place he had stopped Shannon's car that first day. She'd been as feisty as a wild colt, and just as challenging.

As they traveled upward, they began to see more and

more blackened trees where tongues of the fire had surged downward. Some areas remained untouched even though sections of the mountain on both sides had been ravaged. When they reached the spot where her car had gone off the road, he shot a quick look at her. A surge of thankfulness swept through him that she was here with him, safe and well. There had been many blessings in their short time together.

Shannon was thinking along the same lines as she viewed the rocky slope where she had nearly lost her life. A crumpled heap of blackened metal was all that remained of her expensive white sports car. She remembered how devastated she had been. How angry. How resentful that such a thing had happened to her.

"What do you see?" Alice Gordon called from her seat across the aisle.

"Nothing important. Nothing at all," she said when Ward slowed the van at the place where her rented cottage had stood. Only tumbled timbers and charred remains were left to mark the spot. She shivered, remembering her stubbornness in wanting to stay there. When the Gordons' property came into view, there was a collective holding of breath in the van. Then a loud cheer went up from Kenny's parents.

"Praise God."

"Hallelujah."

Their house still stood, untouched by the wildfire. Blackened trees on the slope behind the house showed how close the flames had come. They could see where firemen had cleared all shrubs and wild grass around the house. Evidence of a backburn had left a barren, six-foot-wide strip that had stopped the fire before it reached the house.

"Do you want to take a look around?" Ward asked.

"No. I'm sure they'll let us return before long. Now that we know everything is safe, our worries are over."

Ward turned the van, and they returned to the school. The Gordons were sharing their good news when Gloria and her parents returned from their surveillance trip. They had lost everything.

"We're leaving as soon as the highway is open," Gloria's father said. "My wife's parents live in Denver. We'll stay with them until we decide what to do. You're welcome to come with us, Shannon. We can have you in Denver in a couple of hours."

"Thank you, but I'm staying…at least for a little while."

Ward didn't know what he would have done if she had readily accepted the offer. He'd never thought of himself as a caveman, but he might have thrown her over his shoulder and carried her home.

The ride to the ranch was a silent one. The sun slipped behind the high mountain peaks, and a dusky twilight was settling over the valley. Tired from the exciting outing, Tara had curled up between them and fallen asleep with her head on Shannon's lap. From time to time, Ward and Shannon glanced at each other, waiting for the other to speak.

When the ranch came into view, Ward suddenly pulled over to the side of the road. Lights from the house and stable were like yellow beacons guiding the way home. They could see a scattering of horses slowly moving about in the grassy meadow.

"This is my life, Shannon," Ward said quietly to her. "I left it once, but I'll not leave it again. It's not an easy life. It's not glamorous. It's not even all that profitable as businesses go," he admitted wryly. "Just a lot of hard work. I can't promise you anything more than what I am and what I have. I know you're used to a lot more, and I've tried to tell myself that it wouldn't be fair to…to…" He hesitated.

"To ask me to marry you?"

"Yes. Will you? I love you, Shannon, more than I ever thought possible. Would you make me and my little girl the happiest two people in the world?"

She hesitated, knowing that she had to be honest with him. "I know how much your faith means to you. I've only taken baby steps toward the kind of commitment that is important to you. What about all the warnings you gave me that you would never marry anyone who didn't have faith in God as strong as yours? Wasn't that a criteria for choosing a wife and mother for your child?"

"I was wrong," he answered readily. "None of us have a full measure of faith. We are all on the same path in different places. You can help me grow, and I can help you. That's what we're here for—not to judge each other. I can tell you're seeking the Lord, and that's all that matters." His eyes softened. "I know I'm asking you to give up a lot to marry a cowboy rancher."

"Yes, you are," she agreed, smiling. "I would have to give up things like being lonely, frightened, and trapped. But I think I could get used to having a family who loves me, and a strong, loving man to protect me.

In case you haven't guessed, I'm deeply in love with you, Ward Dawson.''

He leaned across and kissed her. "Is that a yes?"

"Yes!" Tara answered loudly as she lifted her head and her wide-awake eyes snapped with happiness. "Yes, yes, yes."

"I guess that's definite enough," Shannon said, laughing. "I couldn't have said it better."

Ward leaned over, kissed her and whispered how happy she'd made him. Then he chuckled and said, "Let's go home and tell Beth what Tara's getting for her birthday."

Epilogue

One year later

"Whose idea was it to have a big shindig like this?" Ward teased Shannon as the cars pulled into the ranch driveway.

"Yours," Shannon said smugly, lifting her face for a quick kiss.

"Come on, you lovebirds," Beth chided as she joined them and Tara on the patio, setting down more dishes on the picnic table already loaded with food. "Don't you know the honeymoon is supposed to be over after a year?"

"Not ours," Ward answered. "We're going to set a record, aren't we, darling?"

"Absolutely." Shannon smiled, feeling like a bride all over again. They'd been married on this very patio, and the same people who had been invited for that happy occasion were soon to arrive to celebrate their anniversary. She couldn't believe how totally happy she was, how completely head over heels in love with her husband.

As a familiar van pulled into the driveway, Tara shrieked, "Kenny's here." Her ponytail danced in the wind as she raced across the yard.

Shannon smiled at Ward. "Do you think Kenny is bringing her the puppy he promised?"

He chuckled. "I certainly hope so. If he doesn't, she'll raise such a fuss that we'll all have to leave home."

Beth nodded. "That's all Tara's talked about since she heard that Pokey was the proud papa of five puppies."

As Kenny got out of the car, they saw he had something in his arms. Shannon laughed. "He brought it."

Alice and Tom Gordon joined them on the patio, giving hugs all around. The wiggly black-and-white puppy was the image of Pokey, and Kenny smiled proudly as he showed it off.

Remembering the night the little boy had tearfully been hunting for Pokey, Shannon gave him a big hug and petted the tiny pup. "He's almost as nice as Pokey."

"It's a she," Kenny corrected her solemnly. "My dad says she can have puppies when she's bigger."

"Oh, goody," Tara exclaimed. "Now we can raise puppies and horses, too."

Ward was saved from commenting on his daughter's enthusiastic remark by the arrival of Reverend and Laura Cozzins.

The minister and his wife had been frequent visitors

at the ranch during the year, and Ward and Shannon had become a mainstay in the church.

"I brought you something," Laura said in her usual bustling manner. "No, not an anniversary gift," she said, as she handed Shannon a large box.

Shannon looked frankly puzzled, and Ward raised a questioning eyebrow.

"You agreed to be secretary of our women's service group, didn't you?"

Shannon nodded. "Yes, I did."

"Well, here's all the recording books, papers and records of the last five years. We've been passing it around every election, hoping someone would have the know-how to get it organized."

"Well, this little lady is the angel you've been looking for," Ward said proudly. "She's worked miracles with our record keeping. For the first time, we really have a handle on the business end of the ranch."

With her usual frankness, Beth said, "I swear that Ward never really knew how much money was coming in and going out until he married Shannon."

"Guilty as charged," Ward readily admitted. His eyes held a loving glow as he looked at Shannon. "She's a woman of many talents, and I thank the Lord every day for bringing her into my life."

"We all do," his sister agreed.

Tom Gordon cleared his throat. "Well, I have a little surprise for her."

Shannon's breath caught. "Is it—"

"Sure is. Want to take a look?"

"I'm not sure," she said honestly as she held the packet he gave her without opening it.

"Go ahead, honey," Ward urged.

"Maybe I should wait." Shannon hedged.

Kenny's father laughed. "You might as well get used to people looking at your work. In another month, it's going to be all over the place."

His words were not reassuring as she opened the packet and saw her drawings printed on cream-colored stationery. She looked at each sketch with a kind of wonder. Pride mingled with amazement. They were really good.

"Let me see, let me see," begged Tara.

With a self-conscious smile, Shannon passed the stationery around. She had denied her talent for so long that none of this seemed real.

Ward whispered in her ear, "Pretty good doodling."

Tom bragged that he'd been the first one to recognize the commercial value of her sketches and had persuaded her to find a publisher who agreed.

"I guess you'll be pretty busy from now on," Laura said, eyeing Shannon's figure with a speculative eye. "You two wouldn't have some more good news for us, would you?"

Shannon tried not to blush. They had intended to wait until later in the evening to share with everyone their latest blessing. Beth was the only one who knew.

Ward sent Shannon a questioning look, and she nodded. "Tell them."

He really didn't have to say anything. Everybody knew just by looking at them. Teasing and smiling, they clapped Ward on the back and hugged Shannon.

"We're going to have a baby?" Tara gasped.

Shannon sent Ward a worried glance. She couldn't

tell from the look on Tara's face how she was reacting to the news. They should have prepared her, but it was too late now.

Ward knelt and took her hand. "Yes, Shannon's going to have a baby. God is sending you a little sister or brother."

The little girl looked at Ward and at Shannon. Then she smiled and said with childish wonder, "We really are a family now, aren't we?"

* * * * *

Dear Reader,

I chose to set *Hidden Blessing* against the backdrop
of a Colorado forest fire, because it is in times of crisis
that we examine our spiritual beliefs and are open to
change.

The hard shell of ambition and pride that my heroine,
Shannon, has placed around herself begins to crack
when she finds herself a refuge in an evacuation
center without any worldly possessions. The hero,
Ward Dawson, is challenged to bring Shannon into a
relationship with God, but like so many of us, he has
come to his faith the hard way, and he suspects that
Shannon is on the same path. When he tells her that
growing in spiritual faith is not a sprint but a marathon,
I believe that he speaks a truth for all of us.

Please enjoy the excitement, drama and tenderness in
this love story. Letters of sharing are truly welcome.

Leona Karr

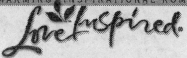